Was It Her?
By Chanel Hardy

Printed in the United States of America.

Hardy Publications

chardypublications.com

ISBN-13: 978-0692058923

"There is no health without mental health; mental health is too important to be left to the professionals alone, and mental health is everyone's business."

-Vikram Patel

Prologue

Nita sat in the back of the ambulance, with the brown soft blanket given to her by one of the paramedics draped over her. She looked down at her indigo sandals, still red and wet from stepping in a mix of her vomit and his blood. Adrian's blood. She found him in the kitchen, his lifeless body laid out on the floor surrounded by a warm pool of his blood. His throat slit from one end to the other, with a large, chef's kitchen knife lodged into his chest, right near his heart. When she walked in and found him lying there, she froze. It was as if her mind couldn't process what she was seeing. Her boyfriend of eight months had been murdered. She slowly walked over to him, her first instinct was to scream, but the vomit, from her being in shock and the overwhelming smell of the blood, came first.

She dropped to her knees and burst into tears. Her screams echoed through the Garcia's two-story home. After getting herself together for a few moments she was able to dig into her back pocket and grab her cell phone to call 911. She panicked with every passing second, her bloody fingers trembling, as she struggled to press the numbers on the screen. She didn't even know what to say, she spent most of the time crying in the dispatcher's ear. By the time the cops came, Nita couldn't even walk without the assistance of the officers. They tried asking her a few questions, but it was no use. She just gave them a dead stare. She had nothing to tell them. She had come over to surprise him. She planned on them spending the evening together watching movies and eating junk food, only to walk in and find him dead.

She stared at the blood on her sandals and the lights from the cop cars flashed all around her. She looked up for a moment and noticed that there was a crowd forming in the street as his body was carried out on a stretcher, covered in white. The blood was so strong, the stains soaked through the sheet, making the sight of him even more horrific. That, combined with all the stares, gasping, whispers, and tears, from neighbors, made Nita feel like throwing up again.

"Amanita!"

She heard her name being called and looked to her right to notice it was her father Robert. Her parents had stopped their car in the middle of the street, not even bothering to park. Her mother and father pushed their way through some of the people that were standing around. Her mother, Latisha, immediately threw her arms around her daughter, accompanied by Nita's father.

"Are you alright? Oh my God! My baby, I'm so sorry!" Her mother exclaimed.

Before Nita could even respond, over walked Detective Loretta Jackson of the Wicomino County Police Department. Nita could tell by the look on her face, she wasn't coming over to say anything good. Loretta stood in front of Nita and her parents, sighing deeply before telling them the last thing they wanted to hear. Nita glanced behind Detective Jackson and noticed a uniformed officer walking up to her, with cuffs in his hand.

"Mr. and Mrs. Matua, I'm sorry, but your daughter is going to have to come with us," Loretta said sternly. "Amanita Matua, you have the right to remain silent..."

Her whole world suddenly went dark as she was being read her rights, and the officer was slapping the cuffs on her wrists. Her father started yelling, demanding that the officer take the cuffs off his daughter and release her immediately. Her mother cried and pleaded with him.

Sixteen-year-old Amanita Matua went from being a normal teenage girl to the number one suspect in the murder of her seventeen-year-old boyfriend, Adrian Garcia within a matter of hours.

1

Moving On

"What do you want!?" She yelled out in terror.

Someone was trying to break into her room, kicking at the door and yanking on the knob. Terrified, Nita had grabbed her dresser and pushed it up against the door to keep out the intruder. It wasn't working. The kicks were getting stronger and it was a matter of time before they were inside. She ran to her window, ripped down the curtains, and flung it open. She climbed out, legs first, knowing there was nowhere to go but down. She would have to jump, which she knew was a bad idea, but it was either jump and risk having a fifty/fifty chance of surviving with a few broken bones or be killed by whoever was after her. She clung to the edge of her windowsill, and within a matter of seconds, she heard her door swing open, knocking over the dresser. The mystery person made their way to the window, grabbing ahold of Nita's hands before she could let go. They then pulled out a huge kitchen knife and impaled her left hand, blood dripping onto her face. She screamed, as the person looking down on her, was Adrian. Except, it wasn't him. He had no face. But she knew it was him because of his dark, thick, wavy hair and sharp widow's peak.

"Adrian?" She said softly, with fear still in her voice.

The faceless being was quiet, still holding on to her as she screamed for her life. He then yanked the knife from her hand, and she couldn't hold on any longer. She fell, falling backward, watching the faceless person watch her fall to her death. This was it.

Amanita awoke to her alarm clock buzzing. It was six-forty-five a.m., and it was her first official day back at school. She rubbed her hand where she had been stabbed in her nightmare, the tingling sensation still lingering. She slammed hard on the "off" button of her alarm clock but decided to lie there for a few more minutes. Her heart was racing from the nightmare she had just had. Strangely this time, she didn't wake up screaming. She had a nightmare every night for the past three months since the night it happened. The night she walked into her boyfriend's home and found him dead on his kitchen floor. It was the worst night of her entire life.

That night of the murder, Nita was placed in handcuffs and escorted to the police vehicle, she watched from the window as her parents continued to plead with the detective to let her go. She couldn't hear anything but muffled sounds of them yelling and screaming at Detective Jackson. Her mother placed both hands up against the windows, calling out to her.

"Nita, sweetie, don't worry! We'll be right behind you! Everything will be okay!" Her mother cried.

The officer pulled away, Nita didn't even bother to look back at her parents who were probably getting back into their car, on their way to the station. Nita's heart repeatedly collided against her chest as she sat in the back of the cold cop car. The leather seats made her uncomfortable, and the doors having no locks from the inside made her feel like she was already a prisoner.

"You think she did it?" The officer sitting on the passenger side whispered to his partner.

"I don't know man."

Nita could see the officer looking at her from the rearview mirror as he was driving. She faced the window, watching the road as they made their way to the police station. She knew for sure that night, that she would be going down for Adrian's murder. She felt like her life was over.

During the interrogation, her father was present, giving the detective murderous looks as his sixteen-year-old daughter was being questioned like a criminal. She sat in that room for five hours, answering the same questions repeatedly.

Why were you at the victim's house?

How long were you there before you dialed 911?

Where were you before you came to the victim's house? Can anyone verify that?

Did you two argue prior to that night?

All questions that she thought would have simple legitimate answers, but Detective Jackson didn't seem convinced. Nita didn't have an alibi. Her parents were out having dinner when she left her house to go see Adrian. Nita was in holding for forty-eight hours, in which it felt like a lifetime before she was released with no charges. Although she had no one to vouch for her alibi, her fingerprints weren't found on the murder weapon. Other than her being at the scene, they had no real evidence to charge her with.

She was free, but this wasn't the end of it. No one, besides her parents and her best friend Benjamin believed she was innocent. Adrian's parents didn't even allow her to go to the funeral, which broke her into pieces. Nita and her parents suffered harassment from the community for weeks. Death threats, vandalism, it was a nightmare. Nita's parents even threatened to sue the police department after Nita attempted suicide until Detective Jackson urged the sheriff to make a public announcement threatening to act against anyone caught harassing the Matua's.

The harassing ceased, and Nita's therapist felt that it was a good time for her to try and get her life back to normal. The first step was getting back to school. She knew this would be the biggest challenge of all. Adrian was a beloved star athlete. The group of friends they once shared, all shunned her and had turned the entire school against her. Thankfully, she had Benjamin. He had done time in Juvie for assault when he was fourteen, so people knew not to mess with him, or Nita if he was around.

Nita heard a knock on her bedroom door, it was her mother Latisha. She must've heard Nita's alarm clock going off. She slowly opened the door and walked over to her daughter's bed, sitting at the edge.

"Big day today sweetie. Are you sure you're ready?" Her mother asked.

"Do I have a choice?" Nita mumbled as she sat up.

"You don't have to do anything you're not ready for."

"I've hidden long enough. I'm tired of giving everyone the satisfaction of isolating myself." Nita said as she tossed her blankets aside and got out of bed.

"Nita! Get your ass down here girl! We got asses to kick today!"

"Oh, I forgot to mention that Benjamin is downstairs waiting for you, probably eating your breakfast." Her mother said playfully.

Nita smiled and quickly made her way downstairs. Sitting in the dining room, Benjamin had one leg propped up, with his medium-length blonde hair in a sloppy man bun and his dirty sneakers on her parent's mahogany table, with a plate in his hand, stuffing his face with crispy bacon.

"Good morning beautiful." He greeted her, mouth still full.

"Morning Ben," Nita replied, yawning.

"You look like crap." He said, putting down the plate and walking up to her. "It's your first day back, you can't show up looking like a human trash can." He ran his fingers through her curly hair.

"I need to shower, then I'll worry about everything else."

Nita's father Robert was coming down the stairs, still in his robe, with his long, wild hair pulled back in a ponytail. His strong Samoan features gave him an intimidating look, even with the long hair.

"I know you didn't have your feet on my table Benjamin." He said, with a tired, gruff voice.

"Good morning to you too, Mr. Matua." Benjamin greeted.

Nita's father didn't always like Benjamin. After Benjamin went to Juvie, Robert forbid his daughter from seeing him. Latisha on the other hand was more empathetic. She grew up with Benjamin's parents and knew he had it rough at home. After Adrian's murder, Benjamin was supportive and there for Nita nearly every single day. Robert got a change of heart and had a newfound respect for the boy. He still didn't

approve of his tough, street ways but Benjamin made his daughter happy, and that's all that mattered.

"My girl! It's a very big day for you, how are you feeling?" He asked,
smiling and walking over to hug his daughter.

"I'm fine. I know it's going to be hard, but I'm ready."

"Good, don't be afraid to come home early if you need too. I'll be
here." He replied.

"I'll be okay; besides, Benjamin won't let anyone give me any trouble."

"Good. That's why I trust him." Her father said, looking at Benjamin for reassurance.

"I love you guys, but I need to shower," Nita said to them, rubbing
her eyes.

"Let me know when you two are ready, I'll drive you to school."
Her father made his way to the kitchen to fix his cup of coffee. "...and
keep your feet off my table Benjamin."

Nita shook her head as Benjamin playfully mocked her father. She
ran upstairs to finish getting ready. After her shower, the thought of going to school was starting to make her nervous again. She got dressed in
a pair of black denim shorts and a yellow cotton t-shirt. She pulled her
long hair up in a bun and grabbed her white flip flops.

As she went back downstairs, her mother was getting ready to head
out the door. Latisha a veterinarian, worked the morning shift at the
local animal hospital while her husband, a firefighter, worked nights at
the station.

"You look, nice sweetie." Her mother complimented her, with a
hair tie in her mouth, pulling her long dreadlocks back into a ponytail.
"I wish I could go with your father to take you to school today, but I
can't be late. Love you though."

"I know mom. Love you too. Get to work, don't worry about me,
I'll be okay, I promise."

Her mother kissed her on the cheek. "Alright then. See you this evening."

She kissed Robert and left, hurrying to her car.

"You don't look edgy enough, where's the makeup?" Benjamin buoyantly asked. He reached into his left pocket and grabbed his midnight black eyeliner. "Put some of this on."

"I'm not wearing that. I'll look like a raccoon."

"Let's go you two." Her father interrupted.

Nita and Benjamin grabbed their backpacks and followed Robert outside. As they walked to the car, Nita noticed her neighbor, Deon, staring at them while he watered his parent's lawn. His eyes, dead on Nita. Deon and Nita used to date before she started dating Adrian. Deon became controlling and jealous, and eventually, Nita grew tired of his childish, misogynistic ways and ended it. She was worried him living next door, would be problematic, but her father made it known that Deon had to stay away from his daughter.

"Can we help you?!" Benjamin shouted.

"Benjamin... don't," Nita warned.

"Let's *go* you two." Her father reiterated.

They all got into the car, Benjamin blowing Deon a kiss, to taunt him.

They arrived at Orchard Valley High five minutes later. Nita scoped out the scene, before getting out of the car. Her stomach started to turn.

"You got this Amanita. Remember, you can come home if you need too." Her father reassured her, his hand on her shoulder.

"I know."

She and Benjamin got out of the car and walked steadily into the building. The stares began. All eyes glued to Nita and Benjamin. As soon as they approached Nita's locker, she noticed someone approaching her from her left. It was Carla Ortega, and she didn't look happy to see Nita.

2

Adrian's Secret

"Look whose back."

"Hello, Carla." Nita greeted, cautiously.

She approached Nita and Benjamin, with Briana and Daniel, her lackeys next to her. At one point they were all friends. Except for Benjamin of course. He hung out with Nita but always avoided the popular cliques. Carla was also Adrian's ex. Although she dumped him, she was still jealous of Nita when they started dating. Carla and Adrian remained friends, so naturally, she had to deal with Nita whether she wanted to or not. She and Nita eventually became friends, of course, that was short-lived once Adrian died. Carla was filled with rage after his death, she hated Nita more than ever.

"Are we going to have a problem?" Benjamin asked, getting defensive.

"Nope. I just came to say hello." Carla replied, gazing up and down at Nita like a predator ready to pounce.

"Okay, well bye!" Benjamin shouted at her.

"What's going on over here?" An adult voice chimed in from close by. It was their English teacher, and the woman who ran the after-school book club twice a week that Nita was in, Ms. Stone. Her classroom was a few doors down from Nita's locker. She walked toward the group of students. "Amanita Matua, it's nice to have you back. All of you need to be heading to class. Now."

"I'll see you in a bit," Benjamin whispered to Nita before walking away, but not before making sure Carla was gone first.

Nita closed her locker and greeted Ms. Stone. "It's nice to be back, thanks."

"I know you've got a lot to catch up on, but I'm looking forward to seeing you at our book club this afternoon. No pressure of course." Ms. Stone smiled.

"I'll try."

"Good, now get to class before you're late." Ms. Stone turned around and walked back toward her classroom, her bright red heels clicking against the marble hallway floor. She was by far one of the prettiest and most stylish teachers at Orchard Valley. Nita leaned against her locker, taking a deep breath before entering her first-period class.

The entire day, Nita got nothing but stares from everyone. At lunch, she and Benjamin sat at a table in the corner, by themselves. She would glance over, and catch Carla looking, and rolling her eyes, making sure Nita saw her, trying to be intimidating. Benjamin saw her, grabbed his butter knife, and made a throat-cutting gesture. Carla, disgusted, grabbed her tray and left, her friends following behind. Nita wasn't afraid of her but didn't want to go the rest of the school year dealing with her nonsense.

Nita's favorite class was Chemistry. Besides English, she also loved science. When the bell rang, her Chemistry teacher, Mr. Nelson asked her to stay behind for a few minutes.

"Ms. Matua, I'd like to speak with you, if you have a moment."

"Sure, Mr. Nelson. What's up?" She asked, moving to take a seat in the front of the classroom.

"I just wanted to see how you were doing, and if you wanted to talk." He got up from his seat to stand in front of the desk, closer to her.

"I'm doing better. My therapist thought it was a good idea that I come back."

"Do you feel like you were ready?"

"Well, I was getting tired of sitting at home, so I'm glad I'm here."

Mr. Nelson walked over to her and placed his hand on her shoulder, "I'm sorry that you weren't allowed at Adrian's funeral. I can't imagine how that must've made you feel."

Nita felt like she was going to cry, but held it in. She didn't want her teacher to see her so vulnerable.

"It was hard but, I got through it."

They were suddenly interrupted by someone opening the door. It was Ms. Stone. "Ed, why are you bothering my star student?" She asked playfully.

"Amanita and I were just catching up Carmen, that's all. Why are you entering my classroom unannounced?" He shot back, in a joking manner.

"I can do as I please, thank you very much." Ms. Stone smiled at him.

Hearing them call each other by first names was weird, but they were dating, so she wasn't surprised by it. Seeing them flirt and be discreetly intimate was like watching an episode of Parks and Rec. They were Ben and Leslie of Orchard Valley. Awkward but adorable.

"Amanita, since you're here, I was wondering if you were still coming to our club meeting?" Ms. Stone asked.

Earlier, Nita had considered it, but after Mr. Nelson's emotional reminder about Adrian's funeral, Nita was no longer in the mood.

"I'm pretty tired. I think I'll skip this one. But you'll see me at the next one. Promise."

"Alright then. No worries. We're reading *The Fire Beneath* by R.M. Stevens. You have that one, right?" Ms. Stone replied.

"Yes, I do. I'll be sure to remember to bring it."

"I think we're done here. I just wanted to check up on you. You're free to go." Said Mr. Nelson.

"Thanks, Mr. Nelson. I appreciate it." Nita grabbed her chemistry book and left the classroom to head to her locker.

Benjamin was waiting there for her, impatiently. "What was the hold-up?" He asked.

"Mr. Nelson just wanted to check on me, that's all." She replied.

Nita then remembered that the book Ms. Stone wanted her to bring to the book club meeting, which was Thursday, was at Adrian's house. She had given it to him because he had promised to read it. She never got a chance to find out if he ever did.

"Ben, we've got to make a stop."

"where?"

She paused, then spoke again, "Adrian's house."

"What? I don't think so! Why do you need to go there?" He demanded.

"The book that I need for book club is there. I know his parents hate me, well, his dad anyway, but I could try."

Benjamin looked at her like she was crazy. "Your first day back in the normal world and you're already taking risks? Oh, I like it."

They turned in the opposite direction and walked to Adrian's house. When they arrived, his father's car wasn't in the driveway. Which was a good sign? He was the one who had forbidden Nita from coming to the funeral. Adrian's mother wasn't as cruel, although she still didn't believe Nita was completely innocent.

Nita and Benjamin approached the house, and Nita immediately got flashbacks from that night. She paused, holding her stomach.

"We don't have to do this," Benjamin told her.

"No, it's fine. I have to." She replied. They walked up to the door, and Benjamin rang the doorbell. A few moments later, Adrian's mom answered. It was no surprise that she was shocked to see Nita.

"Amanita, you shouldn't be here. You know that." She said in a concerned voice.

Nita hadn't spoken to Adrian's parents at all since his death. The last time she saw them was at the police station the night of the murder.

"Hello, Mrs. Garcia. I know I shouldn't be here, but, I'm back in school now, and there are some things of mine in Adrian's room. A book to be specific. I was hoping it would be alright if I could have it."

She looked at Nita suspiciously. Her husband wasn't home, so it wouldn't hurt if Nita just ran inside for a quick second to get her book. Still, Mrs. Garcia was hesitant.

"Please," Nita asked softly.

"Alright but make it quick. He stays outside." She said, referring to Benjamin.

Nita smiled and walked inside. As soon as she walked in, she closed her eyes and ran toward the stairs, trying to avoid looking in the kitchen on her right, as she passed by. As she approached the top of the steps, she walked slowly to Adrian's bedroom. She placed her hand on the doorknob and took a deep breath before entering. Everything was the same as if he was still there. His basketball trophies sat on the shelf to the right. His Lakers posters were still intact. She walked over and sat on his bed. The picture of them that was taken at homecoming still sat on his dresser. She picked it up, reminiscing on the memory. She started to cry, then quickly wiped her tears, as she didn't want to waste too much time before Mrs. Garcia came up.

Her eyes wandered around the room, trying to see where the book could be. Adrian always kept a tidy room, so there wasn't much to look through. She got up and took a quick look through his dresser drawers, under his bed, but no sight of it. She then went to look in his closet. The smell of him still lingered on his clothes. She pushed them out of her way, still no sight of the book, then she remembered about the box. In the back of Adrian's closet, there was a box, where he kept memorabilia from his childhood. But that wasn't all, there was a hidden compartment at the bottom, where he kept his caffeine pills. His parents were health nuts, especially his father being a doctor, so they didn't approve of him taking them.

After looking in just about every place she could think of, she figured there was no harm in searching the hidden compartment. She took everything out of the box and opened the rectangular flap exposing the secret space. There it was, her copy of *The Fire Beneath*. She smiled, thinking of how sweet it was that he treasured her book so much, to keep in his secret place. She then noticed a small blue ball of plastic wrap. She knew they weren't his caffeine pills because the bottle was right next to her book. Her head tilted with curiosity. She picked up the mysterious blue wrapping and examined it. She opened it and couldn't believe what she was seeing. Small, white, circular pills. There was no way these were what she was thinking.

Adrian had drugs? It can't be. He would never.

She heard footsteps coming up the stairs, knowing it was Mrs. Garcia, she quickly grabbed her book. placing everything back into the box, closing it, and stuffing the pills she found into her pocket. She closed the closet door as Mrs. Garcia was approaching the room.

"Did you find your book?"

"Yes," Nita replied, with the book clenched to her chest.

"Good."

Nita could tell by the way that Mrs. Garcia was looking around Adrian's room, that it was best she left now.

"Thank you for letting me come in. I miss him too." Nita put her hand on Mrs. Garcia's shoulder. She didn't respond to Nita's gesture. Nita headed back downstairs, and out the door, where Benjamin was still waiting.

"Took you long enough." He said.

"Shut up and let's go. I have something you need to see."

3

The Hole

They reached Nita's house and immediately ran up the stairs.

"Hi, dad! Bye, dad!" She yelled, as her father sat on the couch eating a bowl of cereal. He barely got a chance to respond before she and Benjamin were both in her room with the door closed. She tossed her backpack on her bed and plopped down next to it.

"Jeez, what's got you all wired up?" Benjamin asked. "...and what is it that you have to show me so badly?"

Nita pulled the blue wrapper containing the pills out of her pocket, with an unsettling look on her face, looking up at Benjamin who was still standing.

"What are those?" He asked.

"I don't know, I was hoping you knew."

He walked closer to her and grabbed them from her hand. "Holy hell! These are rippers!"

"Shhh! Not so loud! What are rippers?"

"Amphetamines."

Nita was confused, and her mind was having a hard time processing this. "Are you sure? That can't be."

"I'm sure, and it is. Your dead boyfriend was taking rippers."

"Benjamin!" Nita shouted, upset at his inappropriate dead boyfriend comment.

"Alright, I'm sorry. But really, why would he have these? I didn't know he was into that."

"He wasn't." Nita's facial expression went from being confused, to sad. "At least, not that I knew of."

Benjamin took a seat next to her, placing his hand on her thigh to comfort her. "Look, it doesn't matter now."

"It does matter. Do you know what this means? Whoever he got these from could've been involved in his murder or know something."

Benjamin didn't like where this was going. "Nita, you've got to let this go. You worked so hard getting things back to normal, you can't go down this road. I won't let you."

"But It wouldn't hurt to ask around."

"Yes, it would." He replied. "I'm throwing these away, you don't need them lying around."

He shoved the pills into his pocket. "Look, I gotta go, I'll call you when I get home. Are you going to be alright when I leave?"

"Yeah, I'll be fine. I'll probably just take a nap."

He grabbed his backpack and headed toward the door. "Nita, don't let this pill stuff get to you. Adrian was a teenager like the rest of us. It's not a big deal." He said.

"You're right. See you tomorrow."

"See ya." Benjamin left, closing the door behind him.

Nita knew she wasn't going to let this go. She knew Benjamin meant well, but he was wrong. Adrian would never take drugs. Sure, he had his caffeine pills, but they weren't anything serious. If he had drugs in his room, then he had to have been holding them for someone. Nita didn't want to believe that he would sell drugs, but right now, anything was better than believing he was using them.

She waited an hour for her father to leave for work and texted her mother to tell her she was hanging out with Benjamin, so she wouldn't worry. Nita needed answers, and the only place she could think of, where she could find someone who could tell her more about the drugs she found, was the Hole.

The Hole was an abandoned house where local kids went to smoke, drink, and do other obnoxious things. It was called the Hole because some years ago, there was a rave being held, and the second floor caved in, injuring at least thirteen people. One even died. Surprisingly, it didn't stop the drunks and the dope heads from hanging out there. It was the last place she wanted to be, but her curiosity wouldn't stop her from going. She tossed her flip flops into her closet and grabbed her sneakers. The Hole was about a ten-minute walk from her house, so it wouldn't take long. She shoved her cell phone into her back pocket, clipped her house keys to her shorts, and left the house as quickly as she could.

When she arrived, there was a couple making out on the front porch. They looked to be around her age, as most were that hung out here. They didn't look familiar, so they didn't go to Orchard Valley. She walked up to them and squeezed past the boy on the left side. They were so into the make-out session, they didn't even bother to look up when she was trying to get by. She opened the door, a whiff of marijuana, cigarettes, and beer hit her in the face. The place reeked of it, and it was disgusting, Nita had to hold her breath. She would've covered her nose and mouth with her t-shirt, but it would've made her look out of place, and she wanted to blend in. She looked up, at the gaping hole above her. She had never actually seen it in person before, only in pictures. It looked even bigger now. All the windows were boarded up, so the place was dark, just smoke filling the air and stoners hanging lazily all over the place. Most of them looked too out of it to notice her, except Max. He came walking toward her from what looked like it used to be the kitchen.

"Nita? Nita, right? What are you doing here?" He asked, confused to see someone like her in a place like that.

"Oh, me? Nothing." She replied, nervously, not knowing what to say.

Max Saunders went to Orchard Valley, but he and Nita only had a few classes together since freshman year. Max usually hung out with the stoner kids, so Nita wasn't surprised to see him there.

"Nothing? So, you're lost then?" He asked, jokingly.

"No, I'm not lost." Nita took a deep breath. "Can I ask you something? Where could I find rippers?"

Max's facial expression was dumbfounded. "What?" He asked, shocked, and confused.

"Rippers? You know ant-"

"Yeah, yeah I know what they are geez! Why do you want to know?"

"I want some," Nita said in a low voice, unconvincingly. She knew he didn't believe her.

Max looked her up and down, trying to understand what a girl like her, a good-girl scholar with strict parents would want with rippers.

"You won't find any here." He told her.

"Well, where?"

Max still couldn't believe a girl like her was asking for drugs. "Look, meet me by the bleachers after school tomorrow. We'll talk, alright?"

"Okay," Nita replied, coughing from all the smoke. Max chuckled at her, shaking his head.

"You should get out of here before you kill yourself."

Nita looked at him, a little embarrassed. "Bye." She said softly as she turned around and hurried out of the house. Max just gave a slight wave, even though Nita had already left. Once she exited the yard, she jogged home as quickly as she could. The entire time she was thinking about her conversation with Max.

Is Max selling rippers? Then he's probably the one that gave them to Adrian!

She didn't know what would happen when they met up after school the next day. If he would sell her the drugs or call her out on her bull. Either way, she felt like she was one step closer to finding the truth about the drugs she found in Adrian's room, which could possibly lead her to the person that really killed him. Thinking about all of this was starting to overwhelm her. When she got home, she immediately ran into the bathroom, turned on the sink, and doused her face with cold water. She thought about what Benjamin had told her earlier, about letting this go. She couldn't. After everything that she had been through, she needed answers. She deserved them, and so did Adrian, and his parents.

She grabbed a towel to dry her face, then went to her room. Her cell phone started to ring, it was Benjamin, but she wasn't in the mood to talk. She texted him and told him she was going to take a nap and would talk with him later. She tossed her phone on her bedside stand and began to undress, changing into her pajamas. Since it was her first day back, she didn't have any homework, which was good because she wouldn't have been able to focus on it anyway.

About twenty minutes later, her mother arrived home from work. Nita was in the kitchen cooking a frozen pizza when she heard her mother coming through the front door, tossing her keys on the nearby table. She walked into the kitchen, her left hand rubbing her neck.

"I'm exhausted, Hey sweetie. How was school?" Latisha asked, walking over to her, giving her a kiss on the cheek.

"It was fine. Carla wasn't too happy to see me, but other than that, besides the stares, no one bothered me at all."

"Oh good. They knew better, Benjamin would tear them a new one." She grabbed a bottle of water from the fridge, chugging it down within seconds. "Where is he anyway? I thought you two were hanging out?"

Nita then remembered about the text she sent her mother earlier. "We were, but something came up at home, so we canceled."

Latisha gave her daughter a worried look. "I hope everything is okay with him."

"It's nothing. His parents probably just got into a fight again, you know, the usual." He said.

Benjamin's home life was very dysfunctional. His father was a drunk, which usually led to verbal and sometimes physical altercations between him, his wife, and his son. The fact that he dealt with that and was still by Nita's side while she dealt with the aftermath of Adrian's death was why she and her mother loved him so much. Her father would never admit it, but he cared for him too.

"Well, I'm glad your first day back was good. I'm gonna go shower, want to watch a movie afterward?"

Nita loved watching movies with her parents, but after today's events, she wanted to be alone. "Maybe tomorrow. I think I'm going to just read and go to bed early."

Latisha looked a little disappointed but respected her daughter's space. "Alright then, let me know if you need anything." She left the kitchen and headed upstairs. Nita pulled her pizza from the oven and took it into the dining room to eat before going back to her room for the evening.

When she got back to her room, she grabbed *The Fire Beneath* and began reading. It was a novel about a woman in 1960's Nigeria, who had been having visions of a demon, which drove her to murder her child, and be sent to an insane asylum. Nita had read the book before giving it to Adrian, so this was her second time reading it. In a strange way, it was comforting, mostly because in the end, it turns out the woman wasn't crazy. Her husband was involved in black magic, setting her up so he could run off with his mistress. The baby she killed wasn't her child and was already dead, killed by the husband. She was set free and reunited with her child. It was one of Nita's favorite books. She read about 4 chapters before turning on her TV and watching some random cartoons before going to sleep.

4

Pinky Promise

Nita sat Indian-style in front of Adrian's tombstone, holding a bouquet of white lilies. She placed the flowers right in the center, where remains of dead Chrysanthemums from previous visits from loved ones had been. He had only been dead for three months, but his tombstone had looked as if he had been dead for centuries. The edges had cracks, the engraving, which read *A beloved son, athlete, and friend* was hardly visible anymore. Tears ran down her face as she stared at his name.

"I'm so sorry. I wish you were here, I miss you so much."

Suddenly, what was just a bright, blue sunny sky, became covered in clouds. It started to thunder, and gusts of wind smacked against her skin. The flowers surrounding his grave started to scatter, blowing in different directions. The wind started to pick up, then it started to rain. It didn't even begin as a drizzle, the rain immediately poured down like a hurricane. Nita noticed that the dirt beneath her started to move. At first, she thought it might've been an insect making its way to the surface. She leaned in closer, touching the soil with her fingertips. A hand, Adrian's hand had burst through the muddy soil and grabbed Nita's throat with maximal force. She wanted to scream but couldn't, her voice was gone as his hand squeezed at her neck tighter and tighter. She grabbed ahold of his arm, desperately trying to break free, but he was too strong. She started to cough and gag as her lungs filled with blood. The ground beneath her got softer, and his hand started to pull her under. It was all happening so fast. Before she knew it, she was being pulled into his grave, her mouth, nose, and eyes filling with dirt. She felt herself take her last breath, before she awoke in her room, screaming, in a bed full of sweat.

"Mom! Dad! Please! Help me please!" She screamed, as her parents burst through the door. Within seconds she realized that it was all just a dream, another nightmare. Her parents rushed over to her.

"Nita, It's alright. It was just a bad dream. We're here." Her mother said in a calming voice.

Nita sat up, crying, her back and hair soaked in her sweat. Her mother gently moved the wet strands of hair out of her face. "I don't think you should go to school today." Which sounded more like a demand than a suggestion.

"You think we should call the therapist?" He asked Latisha. "I think she might need to go back to her daily sessions."

"No!" Nita yelled, interrupting him.

"We'll consider it." Her mother added. "But we won't make you do anything you don't want to do."

"But these nightmares can't continue like this! Look at her!" Robert was getting angry. Not at them, he hated seeing his daughter suffer and wanted to do whatever it took to get her out of it.

"As I said, we'll consider it!" Latisha snapped back at him.

"I'm fine!" Nita snapped at them both. "I'll stay home today, but I don't want to go back to therapy. Please." The last thing she wanted to deal with was her parents arguing in front of her.

Her parents looked at each other, Their faces filled with guilt.

"Alright then. Just let us know if you need anything." Her mother said.

"I'm going to go put on some breakfast, you hungry?" Robert asked Nita.

"No."

"Well, I'll leave it on the stove for you. Yell if you need me, love you."

"Love you too dad."

Robert left her bedroom, and Latisha walked over to follow. "I'm on my way out for work. I'll see you when I get home. Maybe we can talk more about this then?"

Nita nodded in agreement. Her mother gave her a slight smile and left the room. Nita rubbed her hands on her shirt, then through her hair. She felt like she had taken a jump in a swimming pool, and it was gross. She grabbed her cell phone from her nightstand and texted Benjamin that she wasn't going to school. When he asked why she told him about the nightmare. He wanted to come over, but his dad would kill him if he missed school, so he had to go, but he told her he would come over after. She then remembered about Max and knew she still had to meet him after school about the rippers. She got up and went to the bathroom to shower, then head downstairs for breakfast.

Around one-thirty, she got dressed and told her father she was going for a little walk to clear her head. If she had told him she was going to school, he'd start asking questions. She headed toward Orchard Valley and went straight around to the back of the school, toward the football field to wait for Max on the bleachers. School dismissed at two o'clock, so it wouldn't be long. While waiting, she texted Benjamin to let him know she had gone for a walk, since she knew he'd be heading straight for her house when school let out. Within five minutes of the bell ringing, she saw Max heading toward the bleachers from the building. No books in hand, just his black hoodie zipped all the way up with the hood over his head, looking like he was up to some shady business. He ran with a shady crowd usually, so it didn't draw any unusual attention. He noticed Nita and climbed up the bleachers, to the very top where she was sitting.

"You're actually here." He said sarcastically, taking a seat next to her.

"Yeah, I was serious."

"I see."

There was a moment of silence.

"So, you want to know where to find rippers? I still don't see what a girl like you wants with them. Well, actually, I can't say I'm too surprised, with your boyfriend's murder and all."

Nita began to get annoyed. "Can you help me out or not?" She asked, impatiently.

"You need to see someone named Chin." He told her.

"Chin? What kind of name is that?" She asked, with a smirk.

"Don't worry about it. Just go here." Max handed her a torn piece of paper with an address on it.

529 Bakers Rd.

Nita read the address and looked at Max. "I just go here and ask for Chin? What does he look like? Do I need a secret password or something? Is it safe?" She asked, worried, and curious.

"You ask too many questions. Just go there. That's all I can tell you." Max got up and started to climb back down the bleachers.

"Max, wait!" She called out to him.

"What?"

"Thanks."

"Yeah, sure." He continued down the bleachers, jogging back toward the school building. Nita waited a few minutes to leave the bleachers, still looking at the paper he had given her.

Now what? She thought.

She didn't want to buy any drugs, she just wanted to know who sold them. But there was no way she could go to an unknown location, possibly a crack house, asking about drugs but not buying any. She wouldn't live to make it home. As she made her way down off the bleachers, walking to the front of the building through the side, she noticed Ms. Stone outside smoking a cigarette and having a conversation with another teacher, so she tried to blend in with other students walking by, so she wouldn't be seen.

While walking back home, she got a call from Benjamin, most likely calling to see how long she would be out, while he waited at her house for her. She arrived back home to find him sitting on her couch, eating a bag of popcorn.

"About time. You alright?" He asked with a mouth full of popcorn.

"Yeah, I'm fine. Let's go upstairs." She proceeded toward the stairs, and he followed, popcorn still in his hand. As soon as they got inside her room, she closed the door, standing with her back up against it, facing Benjamin who was sitting on her bed, still munching on the popcorn.

"Promise not to be mad?" She asked, biting her bottom lip.

Benjamin stopped chewing and glared at her. "What did you do now?" He asked, in a concerned tone of voice.

Nita took a very deep breath. "I went to the Hole yesterday after you left. I wanted to see if I could find out anything about the drugs. I ran into Max, and he told me to meet him after school, then he gave me an address to go see someone named Chin who I'm guessing sells rippers. I didn't tell him why I wanted them. I know you told me to leave it alone, but I couldn't."

"Nita! Are you crazy!" He snapped.

"Not so loud! My father will hear you."

"I don't care! What do you think you're doing? You went to the Hole, alone! Then talking to Max? He's a freak!" Benjamin was furious.

"I'm sorry. I just needed answers." She said, feeling horrible for making him upset. She knew he was only looking out for her.

"Well, what now? You got this address, what do you think is going to happen if you go to this place? They're just going to welcome you with open arms? You won't last five minutes! I won't let you go."

Benjamin was right. She barely blended in when she went to the Hole, she just got lucky that the people there were too high or drunk to notice.

"I was hoping... you could go with me?" She said, hesitantly.

"Nope. No way." He sat there, arms crossed.

"Please?" Nita begged. "I've got a hundred bucks. All you've got to do is buy some rippers for me. I'll just stand there, quietly. I just want a face, that's all."

"No!"

Nita was done begging. "I'm going with or without you."

Benjamin let out a huge sigh, rubbing his temples. "Nita..."

"I mean it!" She interrupted.

"Fine!" He yelled.

She smiled, jumping up to give him a huge hug. "Ben, I know you think I'm crazy, but you out of all people should understand why I can't let this go."

"I know. I just don't want you getting yourself hurt or killed." He broke their embrace, looking into her eyes. "So, you get to see this person, Chin, or whatever. Then what? You go to the police? With drugs, you bought from the drug dealer? How do you even know if this is the person that sold Adrian the drugs?"

Nita realized she hadn't thought all of this through. "I don't know yet. I'll figure it out when the time comes. Right now, I just need to do this."

Benjamin didn't like the idea of doing any of this, but he knew that she was serious when she said she would go with or without him, so he had no choice but to help her.

"After school tomorrow. We'll go then. I can borrow my mom's car." Benjamin told her.

"Alright. Sounds good." She agreed to the plan.

"After this, we're done with this stuff."

"Yeah, sure," Nita replied, not sounding too convincing.

"I'm serious." Benjamin made her pinky promise.

She wrapped her pinky finger around his. "Promise."

5
Chin

Nita stood by her locker after her final class had dismissed, putting her books away. As she moved her calculus book, a photo of her and Adrian fell out of her locker and landed at her feet. She picked it up, and it was a photo of him at one of his basketball games. The Orchard Valley Knights won by 10 points that night. Adrian looked amazing. Before she could even put the photo back into her locker, someone had walked up and snatched it right out of her hand. It was Carla of course, looking like she was ready to start some trouble.

"What the hell? Give me my picture back!" Nita demanded.

"Or what?" Carla teased. She looked at the photo, putting on a menacing smirk. "I was with him that night, before his game. He told me he still loved me."

Nita laughed, not because she thought it was funny, but because she couldn't believe Carla had the nerve to approach her with this nonsense. "Whatever helps you sleep at night Carla, now give me back my picture, and get out of my face. I'm not in the mood to deal with you today."

Carla got closer to Nita's face. "I know it was you." She whispered. "I know you did it. Everyone knows. You may have fooled the cops, but I'm not stupid."

Nita has livid now. She closed her locker, and locked eyes with Carla, who had officially crossed the line. "You don't know a damn thing, now get out of my face, before I hurt you."

"What are you gonna do, huh? You gonna kill me like you did Adrian?! *Asesino!*" Carla spit, which landed right on Nita's left sleeve.

Not even three seconds later, Carla was on the floor, blood gushing out of her nose from the heavy punch to the face Nita had delivered after that disrespectful, disgusting spit. Carla held her nose in shock, as students started to gather around, holding their phones out, ready to record. Carla got up and immediately defended herself pushing Nita up against the locker, attempting to strike back. But she was no match for her. Nita was skinnier but taller than her which gave her an advantage. Nita had also grown up with male cousins and a tough father, so it all came naturally to her. Carla grabbed Nita's hair, her perfect ponytail coming undone. Nita got one last smack across Carla's face before Mr. Nelson came running through the crowd of students to break up the fight.

"Hey! Cut it out! Now! Both of you!" He grabbed Carla and pulled her behind him. Nita willingly stopped, watching Carla try to get past Mr. Nelson to get back to her.

"You, go to my classroom, now!" He told Nita. "Carla please calm down, I'm taking you to the nurse." He forcefully escorted Carla away and Nita walked quickly to his classroom, pushing through the students still standing around.

She reached his classroom, which was still empty. She took a seat in one of the front row desks. A few minutes later, Mr. Nelson had returned, giving Nita a frustrated look of disappointment, as he fixed his tie and walked over to her.

"Amanita, I expect better from you."

"She started it! She spat on me!" Nita yelled.

"I know you two aren't the best of friends but punching her was unacceptable. You're better than that."

Nita sucked her teeth and folded her arms. "Whatever."

Mr. Nelson felt a little guilty, knowing it was true that Carla was in the wrong first. "I know these past few months have been rough for you. Is there anything you want to talk about? You missed school yesterday, it was only your second day back."

"I'm fine." She replied.

"So, there's nothing bothering you at all?"

Nita felt like Mr. Nelson was getting a little too comfortable meddling in her business. Before she could say anything else, Mr. Nelson had gotten a phone call. He pulled out his cell and judging by his facial expression, it didn't look like anyone he wanted to talk to.

"I gotta take this. Will you excuse me?" He said, sounding not so enthusiastic.

"Actually, I've got to go. Do you mind?"

"Yeah, sure. I'll see you tomorrow. Stay out of trouble Ms. Matua."

He quickly walked out of his classroom to answer the phone call before it stopped ringing. Nita immediately walked out, rushing outside to meet Benjamin. She had reached the front of the building, looking around for him once she got outside, noticing a black Nissan Sentra pull up near the curb. It was Benjamin, who must've skipped his last period class, so he could get his mom's car and be there to meet Nita as soon as school had dismissed. Nita walked up to the car, opening the passenger side door and getting in immediately.

"What happened to you?" He asked, referring to her hair, which was still a mess form her fight with Carla.

"Got into a fight, with Carla."

Benjamin's eyes grew big, his mouth wide open in surprise. "No way! Oh man, and I missed it! Did you kick her ass?"

Nita looked at him, proud to boast about how she took down Carla. "Of course. You know she can't fight. Girls like her never can."

They both laughed, as Benjamin pulled off. "Are you sure you want to do this?" He asked, referring to their plans of going to the address Max had given her.

"Yes," Nita replied, her smile from laughing just a few moments ago had turned into a blank expression. Benjamin didn't say anything else, just nodded.

The location was about 15 minutes away. Once they located the exact address, which was an apartment building, Benjamin decided to park around the corner. Nita fixed her hair, tying it up into a bun while they began walking. The building was decent looking. It wasn't as run down as Nita was expecting. As they approached the door, there was a list of unit numbers with buzzers. She suddenly realized that the address Max had given her, didn't have a unit number. There was no way for her to know which door it was once they got inside.

"Great! He didn't tell me it was an apartment building! Now what?" She said, frustrated.

"I'm going to take a wild guess and say this is where we need to go." Benjamin pointed to the one unit which had black duct tape over the number 202. You could tell based on the order listing of the units. Before Nita could respond, he had already pressed the buzzer.

"What?" A raspy male voice said loudly through the speaker.

Nita and Benjamin looked at each other, trying to figure out who would answer.

"Hello!" The male voice shouted.

"We're here to see Chin." Benjamin finally answered. There was a pause for a few seconds. Nita was beginning to think they had made a mistake and picked the wrong unit.

"Hello?" Benjamin called out, thinking they were being ignored.

"Come up." The male voice said.

They suddenly heard a click, and the door became unlocked. They walked inside, and the light in the hallway was so bright Nita had to put her hand over her eyes. They walked up to the second floor, and 202 was the second door on the right. Before either one of them could knock, the door flew open, and a pale, short white guy with a shaved cut was facing them.

"Get in." It was the same voice they heard over the speaker outside.

Nita and Benjamin didn't hesitate. They made their way inside and the apartment was empty. Nita was expecting it to be like what she saw at the Hole, but it just looked like a normal apartment. Clean, a dark brown leather sofa with a matching love seat. A coffee table in the center of the room with an ashtray full of cigarette butts. There were no pictures on the walls, which was to be expected, considering what type of business went on there.

"Names." The pale man demanded.

"I'm Ben, and this is Nita."

The man walked over to pat them down. First Benjamin, then Nita. Having some stranger's hands all over her, made her uncomfortable, but she knew it had to be done, so she allowed, not budging.

"Follow me."

He led them to one of the bedrooms. Without saying another word, he opened the door, gesturing for them to go in. As they walked in, he closed the door behind them. A Mexican woman with long honey blonde hair sat near the window, smoking a cigarette. Nita and Benjamin looked a bit surprised, as they were expecting Chin to be a man.

"I know you." She said, looking directly at Nita. "I remember seeing you on the news. That girl that killed her boyfriend. Adrian, right?" The woman said his name with such confidence, which made Nita nervous, but curious.

"You knew him?" Nita asked.

"Don't worry about who I know." The woman answered, getting up from the chair and walking over to them.

She wore black stilettos with black leather pants and a pink lace bralette. She reminded Nita of strippers she had seen in music videos. "How many do you want?" She asked, still looking at Nita, referring to the drugs.

"Four is fine," Benjamin answered.

"¡ trae las cosas! Cuatro!" She yelled out to the man who had let them in. "We're finished here. He'll take care of you."

The man had opened the door. Nita and Benjamin began to walk out, not saying a word to the woman. Nita stopped before leaving the room.

"I didn't kill him," she told the woman.

The woman stared at Nita, dead in her eyes, letting out a low, wicked laugh. It was intimidating as hell. "Little girl, run home to mama now."

Nita didn't say anything, she just left, closing the door behind her. In the living room, Benjamin did the exchange with the short man. They got four rippers for $80. They quickly left, not wanting to spend another minute in that place. When they got outside, walking around the corner to get back to the car, Nita looked up, facing the bedroom window to the apartment. The woman was looking out of the window, still smoking a cigarette. She was looking at them both, but Nita couldn't help but feel like the woman's focus was on her. It was weird as if she knew they would be walking in that direction to the car. After a few seconds, she closed the curtain and left the window. When they got into the car, Benjamin had a worried look on his face.

"What's wrong? Everything went well, don't you think?" Asked Nita.

"Don't you think it's odd?" Benjamin asked.

"What do you mean?"

"If that woman was really Chin, why were we able to get to her so easily? Why did Max even send you here? They have people to do this stuff for them. Why did we need to come here to buy rippers?"

"What does it matter? We got them, and we saw who this Chin person is. You heard her, she knew Adrian. This can't be a coincidence."

"She didn't actually say she knew him. His murder was all over the news. Anyone could recognize you or know his name." Benjamin sounded bothered. Nita could tell that this visit was rubbing him the wrong way.

"It's done now. When I get home, we can flush the drugs. Let's just go." She said.

Benjamin pulled off without saying another word. The drive back to Nita's house was silent. She thought about what would happen after this. She knew she couldn't just go to the police, but she also wasn't about to let Chin walk free.

NITA AWOKE TO A KNOCK on her door. Her alarm for school hadn't even gone off yet. She lifted herself up, rubbing her eyes. "I'm up." She said, knowing it was her mother.

Her mother walked in, closing the door behind her. "Nita, I wanted to talk to you before you got ready for school. She sat at the edge of the bed. Nita grabbed her cell phone to check the time. She still had thirty minutes before she had to be up and getting ready.

"Okay, about what?" Nita asked, barley awake. Her mother, with her hand over her mouth, was trying to hold back tears before she spoke.

"Mom, what's wrong?" Nita became more alert as she noticed her mother was upset about something. She knew it was bad news.

"You know that boy, Max. Max Saunders, right?"

Nita immediately felt a pain in her stomach. Wondering why her mother was asking about Max.

"He umm... died last night. A drug overdose apparently. They're saying it was a suicide. I got a text this morning, then saw it on the news not too long afterward."

Nita clasped her hands over her mouth in shock. She couldn't believe it. She had just seen him when they met on the bleachers. She didn't know enough about him to know if he was using drugs, but this wasn't good, and she knew it.

"What kind of drugs, did they say?" Nita was trying to hold back tears herself.

"Painkillers, can you believe that? That poor boy, his poor parents. They didn't even know he was using." This made her mother more emotional, mostly because Nita, had also attempted suicide not too long after Adrian's death. Hearing about another teenager, and someone they knew committing suicide made it personal. "I know you two weren't really friends but, I wasn't sure how this would affect you, going to school today."

Nita was hurting but was trying her best to be strong in front of her mother. She felt guilty, knowing that it had something to do with her. It couldn't have just been a coincidence. If his parents didn't know he was abusing painkillers, then there is a good chance he wasn't, which meant his death was no accident.

"Mom, can you excuse me. I need a moment alone, to process this."

"Sure honey. Just let me know if you need us."

Her mother got up and left the room slowly. Max's death had brought back painful memories Nita wished her parents didn't have to think about. Nita grabbed her cell phone and called Benjamin, pacing her room waiting for him to pick up.

"I heard," Benjamin said, sounding afraid.

"Oh my god! What do I do? It's all my fault isn't it?" Nita was crying.

"Calm down. You didn't do anything, they said it was an overdose."

"You and I both know that's bull!"

"Look, we can't discuss this over the phone. Just get ready for school and I'll be at your house in a bit. Just stay calm, alright?"

"Okay, bye."

Nita hung up and crawled back into bed, pulling her covers up to her chin. She felt like this was the start of something bad, but she had no proof. He could've easily killed himself, just as easily as he could've been murdered. Nita felt dizzy, grabbing the trash can by her bed and vomiting. She was in no mood to go to school but knew she couldn't miss it.

6

Death of a Knight

"Good morning staff and students of Orchard Valley High. I'm sure you all have heard the news of Max Saunder's unfortunate passing last night. We are all saddened by the news. If anyone needs any emotional support, or just someone to talk to, Ms. Stone will be having a student group therapy session this afternoon at 2:45 pm. Thank you all and have a wonderful day."

Principal Morris sounded like he was reading a script as he did the morning announcements regarding Max's death. Students didn't even stop to listen like they did when Adrian died. No one seemed affected at all. When Adrian died, you could feel the loss in Principal Morris's voice. His words were authentic. This time, it just sounded like he didn't really care, and was obligated to tell everyone a random student killed himself. Max may not have been popular or well-loved like Adrian, but he deserved better than this. He was a human being too. As Nita walked to her locker, she noticed a locker with a plastic dollar store flower taped to it. It must've been Max's locker, probably put there by one of the kids he hung out with. It was nice to see someone cared.

Nita sat in English class, everyone having side conversations with one another waiting for Ms. Stone to come in. A few kids made glances at her, in the middle of their conversations. Not that it wasn't normal. No one except Benjamin talked to her. Max had been the only person other than teachers, and her encounters with Carla who had spoken to her at all. Somehow, the silent treatment felt worse than being bullied. Suddenly Nita's cell phone vibrated, it was a text message. She didn't recognize the number but opened it anyway.

I know who you are, and what you're doing.

Stop now.

This is your one and only warning.

"Alright everyone, silence please." Ms. Stone had walked in.

Nita, sitting near the front had no time to react before stuffing her phone back into her pocket.

"Before we start, I just want to inform you all that I will be having a group therapy session in the library this afternoon if anyone wants to come." Said Mrs. Stone

She must've canceled her book club meeting to do this, which was thoughtful of her. Nita had always liked Ms. Stone for that reason. She was sweet, smart, and cared for her students. Principal Morris probably wouldn't have had a therapy session for Max's death if she hadn't volunteered to do it. Ms. Stone's eyes moved to Nita as she spoke as if she was giving a hint for her to come. She noticed Nita had a strange look on her face and became concerned.

"Amanita, are you alright?" She asked.

"May I be excused to use the restroom?"

"Sure, just make it quick."

Nita got up and walked toward the door, running to the restroom one she got outside the classroom. She burst through the door, running into the first stall. Her heart was beating fast, and she felt like she was going to be sick. She went back to the text message and read it over again. Someone knew. They knew about her finding the rippers, looking into Adrian's death, meeting with Max, Chin, everything. Therefore, Max was killed. For helping her. She started to panic and text Benjamin, telling him to meet her after class on the football field. She went to the sink to splash water on her face, to calm herself, then head back to class.

As soon as Ms. Stone's class let out, Nita tried to hurry to the football field, but Ms. Stone stopped her.

"Amanita, wait." She walked over to her. "Do you have a second?"

Nita wasn't in the mood for another teacher-student sit down, but she stayed anyway. "I've really got to go."

"What's got you in such a hurry? You look like you've just seen the boogeyman." Ms. Stone asked, with a smile. "I don't want to hold you up, I just wanted to see if you were going to the group therapy this afternoon?"

Nita raised her eyebrow. "Why would I go? I hardly knew him."

"I just thought it would be good for you, also, I know how triggering death can be for some, and I think it would be nice for the others attending to see someone who, well, understands what they're going through."

"No one understands what I'm going through."

Ms. Stone was beginning to feel bad for asking. "My apologies, I didn't mean-"

"I'll be there." Nita really liked Ms. Stone and knew she meant well. She didn't really want to go but figured it wouldn't hurt just to show up, even for a few minutes.

"That would be lovely." Ms. Stone said politely, with her hand on Nita's shoulder.

"I've really gotta go." Amanita said with urgency.

"Alright, see you this afternoon." Mrs. Stone replied with pressed lips.

Nita left the classroom, hurrying down the hall and out the back doors of the building. She jogged toward the field as she could see Benjamin impatiently waiting.

"What now?" He asked, knowing it wasn't anything good.

"Someone knows. They know everything." Amanita said.

She pulled out her cell phone, pulling up the text message, and showing it to him. As he read it, fear was all over his face. He knelt, trying to take it all in.

"Oh man, oh man... This... This isn't good." Ben took in a deep breath. "I knew we shouldn't have ever gone to that place."

"What do we do now?" Amanita asked.

"What do you mean?! We don't do anything! What part of that message didn't you get?!" His voice grew louder. "This is over! I don't

care what you think happened to Adrian! We are letting this go, now!"
Benjamin was furious.

"Should I go to the police?"

"Are you crazy?! No! They gave you a warning, are you trying to get
yourself killed?! Or me?!"

Benjamin had to take a seat on the ground to calm his nerves. Nita
took a seat next to him. He looked at her with sad eyes. He didn't mean
to blow up at her like that.

"I'm sorry okay. I just want this to be over. They said it was a warning, which means they won't do anything if you stop trying to go after
them. Whoever it is." He said.

"It's got to be Chin right? Who else could it be?"

"I don't know, and don't care." Benjamin stood back up. "Let's get
to class. Just delete that message ok, let's just pretend this never happened."

Nita got up as well. "Oh, I'm going to the group therapy this afternoon, so don't wait for me."

Benjamin gave her a confused look. "Why?"

"Ms. Stone wants me to go, I probably won't stay long."

"Suit yourself." Benjamin put his arm around her and they walked
back toward the building.

IT WAS TWO-THIRTY-FIVE p.m., as Nita checked her cell phone,
sitting in the library waiting for the session to start. So far there was only one other person there besides her. A boy, someone she recognized
but didn't know. She had texted her father, letting him know she would
be staying after. About a minute later Ms. Stone walked in, and three
more people showed up right behind her. The other students took seats
to the left and right of Nita, while Ms. Stone sat facing all of them.

"I'm glad you all decided to come." Ms. Stone began.

"I know it's been a very mournful day, with the unfortunate passing of Max last night."

"It's bullcrap! All of it!" A boy sitting to the left of Nita said angrily. It was the boy who had arrived when she did, before all the others. Based on his faded dark blue hoodie, torn sneakers, and sluggard appeal, he was probably one of Max's friends. Ms. Stone looked at him, caught off guard by his sudden outburst.

"David, right?" She asked, her face locked on him. "It seems like there is something you need to get off your chest. Feel free to share."

"Max wasn't no drug head! He'd never kill himself!" He sucked his teeth. "It just doesn't seem right man."

Nita didn't blame him, If Max's own friends didn't believe he would commit suicide, why would anyone?

"David, I know it's hard to believe that someone you care about would take their own life, but these things happen." Ms. Stone said to him. She glanced over at Nita. "Amanita knows more about that than anyone here, don't you Amanita?"

Nita's eyes shot at Ms. Stone. She couldn't believe it. How did she know about Nita's suicide attempt? More importantly, why would Ms. Stone, a teacher, authority figure, and someone she admired, reveal such an intimate thing about her personal life. It was beyond inappropriate and just humiliating.

"What?" Nita replied to her in a low voice, looking around as the other students were looking at her.

"I know Adrian's death took a toll on you mentally and emotionally, and I just figured that maybe everyone here would like to hear your story."

"How did you know about that!?' Nita's voice grew louder.

"I know this is hard for you to talk about, but this is a safe place. Anything discussed in this room will stay in this room." Ms. Stone could sense that Nita was getting upset, so she tried to speak calmly.

"Losing a loved one is a very common reason for someone to take their own life."

"I didn't try to take my life because of Adrian! Everyone in this stupid town was verbally, physically, and violently harassing me and my family! Everyday! I couldn't take it anymore!"

Nita was infuriated. Everyone was staring at her like she was a psychopath as if they didn't already think she was. Ms. Stone was a fool to think this wouldn't spread around the school by tomorrow. Everyone would know now.

"I'm leaving." Nita got up without even saying another word, or looking at anyone, and stormed out.

"Amanita, wait!" Ms. Stone called out to her.

Crying, Nita ran out of the library, and down the hallway to get out of the building as fast as she could. Running home, she couldn't help but think about the betrayal of Ms. Stone, exposing what happened to her in front of everyone. She also never told Amanita how she knew about it. Nita didn't want to believe that her parents would say anything or Benjamin. The night it happened, they didn't even call the paramedics. Nita's mother had a nursing background and was able to aid her daughter after her near-death experience. Thankfully, Benjamin got to her not long after she took the pills. She was able to throw them up and avoid a trip to the hospital.

Nita reached her house, wiping her face, and fixing herself up before going inside. She didn't want her father to see her upset and ask what was wrong. Before she pulled out her keys to unlock the door, she paused. After everything that had happened today, she felt like she needed to talk to someone. Someone who wasn't a family member or friend. Max's death had been weighing heavily on her all day long, especially after the text message, which was bringing back thoughts and feelings of Adrian's death. She thought that maybe going to the police station to talk to Loretta, it would give her a sense of security, and release. During the investigation, Detective Loretta Jackson was the only one who seemed to not give Nita a hard time. Nita quickly backed away from the front door and started walking back the way she came. The police station was about a twenty-minute bus ride from where she lived. She didn't want to text Benjamin for a ride because she didn't want him to know where she was going. She walked two blocks to the bus stop and caught the 26B to Durango avenue, where the station was located.

Once she arrived, she walked inside, to the front desk where a tall, fat male officer was sitting and asked him if she could speak with Detective Jackson. The man didn't even look up, his face buried in paperwork.

"She's busy." He answered.

Nita knew Detective Jackson would clear her whole schedule if she knew she was there. "Tell her it's Amanita Matua, and it's important."

The man looked up, realizing who she was after she told him her name. "Oh, it's you." He said in an unsympathetic tone.

He picked up the phone to dial her office extension, letting her know Nita was there. He hung up the phone seconds later, letting Nita know Detective Jackson would be out in a minute. Nita waited by the desk, and no longer than two minutes later, Detective Jackson was walking toward her, with a steaming hot cup of coffee in her hand. She had lost a little bit of weight since the last time Nita had seen her, which was months ago. She had even cut her hair in a nineties Halle Berry style. It went well with her chocolate brown skin and new weight loss.

"Hello Amanita, I'm surprised to see you here. What can I do for you?"

"I was hoping I could talk with you." Nita glanced over at the fat man sitting at the desk, eyeing her like he wanted to slap his cuffs on her and throw her in a cell. "In private." She urged.

"Of course, follow me."

Detective Jackson led Nita to her office, which felt like it took forever with the eyes of everyone they walked past glued to Nita. It was like the night she was arrested all over again. Detective Jackson opened the door to her office, gesturing for Nita to take a seat in the hard, brown chair while she walked over to her desk and took a seat.

"What brings you here today Ms. Matua?" She asked, taking a sip from her cup.

Nita didn't even know where to begin. "I was wondering if you had any new information regarding Adrian's case?"

Detective Jackson paused in the middle of taking another sip of her coffee. "You know Adrian's murder has become a cold case. Even if I did, you know I can't give you any of that information."

"I understand. It's just, with the recent death of my friend Max, it just had me thinking about Adrian."

"Yes, Max Saunders suicide. Sad situation. I didn't know you two were friends, sorry about your loss."

"Thank you. I just can't believe he would kill himself." Nita was using Detective Jackson's sympathy to fish for any clues regarding Max's suicide.

"Yes, well, it was a very unfortunate site. The poor boy had to have swallowed an entire bottle of oxytocin. Some were even stuck in his throat. He must've had some serious demons." Detective Jackson shook her head.

Stuck in his throat? Oh my God.

The thought of it gave Nita the chills. Then she realized, pills would get stuck if they were being forced down. It all became even more clear now. Whoever killed Max, forced those pills down his throat, making it look like a suicide. Max was murdered, and the guilt started to overwhelm her again.

"Well, thanks for giving me your time. I'm gonna go." Nita said, getting up from the chair.

"It was nice seeing you Amanita. It looks like you're doing better, that's good."

Nita smiled and began to walk out of her office.

"Oh, and Amanita, if we ever find who killed your boyfriend, I promise you'll be getting a call from me." Detective Jackson returned the smile. Nita quickly left her office and out of the station, hoping to catch the next bus coming by.

As she walked toward the bus stop, she could see the bus up ahead. Now, she contemplated whether she would tell Benjamin about Max. After the text, he made it clear that he wanted all of this to end, and he'd be pissed if he found out she went to the police station. She had no idea what to do now.

7
The Ones You Love

Nita stood in a dark room. It was pitch black. She walked around with her hands stretched out forward, trying to feel for something, anything. There was nothing. No tables, chairs, nothing. It was so quiet, she could hear her heart beating.

"Hello? Is anyone here?"

She knew she was alone. She felt up the wall, trying to feel for any sign of an exit. Still, there was nothing. Suddenly, the room became lit with a bright light. Too bright, she had to close her eyes and allow herself a moment to adjust. When she opened her eyes, she saw blood. Dried blood stains were smeared all over the walls. Gallons of it, everywhere. Nita crouched down on her knees, with her hands over her face. She just wanted to go home. As she pulled her hands away from her face, there was blood. Her hands started to tremble, as she felt all over her face for a wound, confused about where the blood had come from. She started screaming.

Nita woke up in her bed. This time, she wasn't screaming, or in panic. She was just confused. Out of all the bad dreams she had, this one just felt odd. She rubbed her eyes and grabbed her cell phone from her nightstand to check the time. It was almost time for her to get up for school. She crawled out of bed and sluggishly walked to the bathroom to take a shower.

After her shower, she went back into her bedroom to check and see if she had any messages from Benjamin. He'd usually text her that he was on his way over, but this time there were no messages from him. They texted each other last night after she got back home from her visit to the police station. She was waiting until the walk to school to tell him about it. She wasn't going to at first but felt that he needed to know about what she heard from the detective regarding Max's death. She got dressed, grabbed her cell phone, and went downstairs to get breakfast and to see if Benjamin had maybe shown up already. Her parents were in the kitchen, her mother making her plate, and her father fixing his cup of coffee.

"Good morning beautiful!" Her father greeted as she walked near the kitchen.

"Hey, honey!" Her mother replied.

Nita peeked into the dining room, and over to the couch hoping to see Benjamin stuffing his face like he always did. She didn't see him and became a little concerned.

"Benjamin's not here? That's weird. He hasn't texted me since last night." Nita said to her parents, walking up to the counter to grab her plate.

"Good, we can enjoy our breakfast in peace." Her father said.

"Robert hush." Her mother nudged him in his side. "He's probably on his way now." She said to Nita.

"Then he would've texted me by now." Nita looked at her cell phone, still no messages. She decided to text him to ask where he was.

"He'll be here, don't worry yourself over nothing. Now come eat." Her father told her.

She ate her breakfast, standing at the counter glancing at her phone every few seconds waiting on a reply. She finished her breakfast and tossed her plate into the sink. seven minutes had gone by and he still hadn't replied. There was no way he hadn't seen it by now. She decided to call him, but his phone went straight to voicemail. That was impossible unless his phone was dead, which he would never allow. Nita started to get a nervous feeling in her stomach. His parents no longer had a landline, so the only other way to contact him was by calling his parents. She wouldn't in a million years call his dad, but his mother Susan was nice. She went into the living room and dialed Susan's number. It rang five times, and right before Nita hung up, Susan answered.

"Hello."

"Hi, Mrs. Rutner, it's me Amanita. Sorry to bother you, I was just checking to see if you knew where Benjamin was. He's usually here by now but I haven't heard from him all morning. I know it's silly, but I was getting a little worried."

Susan's voice sounded raspy. "We're at the hospital. Something happened to Ben."

Nita felt her heart skip a beat, as her cell phone fell to the floor. *This can't be happening. Not him, not Ben. Oh God, not Ben.*

"Mom!" She yelled out. Her parents rushed in to see what was wrong. Nita was crying, holding her stomach which felt like it was in knots.

"What's wrong? What happened?" Robert noticed the cell phone on the floor and picked it up. Susan was still on the line.

"Hello?" He said. They couldn't hear anything but based on her father's reaction as he talked to Susan, she didn't want to.

"What is it? Who is that?" Latisha asked in a demanding tone. Trying to comfort Nita who was still crying.

"We'll be right there," Robert said to Susan before hanging up. "It's Benjamin. His mother says he was beaten badly late last night. Whoever did it, caught him while he was taking the trash out."

"Oh my God!" Latisha was aghast. "Who would do such a thing?!"

"I don't know, but we need to get up there fast." Said Robert.

Robert grabbed the car keys and they immediately left for the hospital, getting there as quickly as they could. When they arrived, they went directly to Benjamin's room, where his mother and father were waiting outside his door. His mother, eyes red from crying and his father, just standing there looking angry. Latisha immediately went to comfort them.

"You know who did this, don't you?" Benjamin's father Roy said to Nita. "My son is a good kid, he has his problems, yeah, but he wouldn't hurt nobody." The anger in Roy's voice was sharp.

"Hey now, don't you accuse my daughter of anything." Robert approached him, ready to defend his daughter.

"Not now you two," Latisha said hastily.

"I'm sorry I didn't call you sooner," Susan said to Nita. "It was so much going on. It all happened so fast." Susan started to cry again.

"It's going to be alright. How is he now?" Latisha asked.

"He's stable. Badly bruised ribs, nose and hand broken. A swollen eye and one of his teeth were also knocked out. Doctors also said he had some internal bleeding." Susan could hardly finish, pain seeping through her voice. "Two men in masks approached him as he was taking out the trash. By the time we heard the commotion outside they were already gone. I just found him, lying there."

They all stood there, faces full of sadness as they listened to her tell what had happened. Nita walked into his room, not even asking permission first, even though she didn't care if she needed too. He was lying in the bed, unconscious, but he looked peaceful. Probably full of morphine. His face and hand bandaged up, his right eye swollen, just like his mother said. She walked closer to his bedside and grabbed his hand. It broke her heart seeing her best friend like this.

"I'm so sorry Benjamin. I am. I did this to you, I know it." She whispered to him, as tears rolled down her cheeks. "I should've listened to you the first time."

Her parents walked in soon after, Latisha going around to the opposite side of Benjamin and Robert standing next to Nita.

"Poor thing." Latisha grabbed his other hand. Benjamin was like a son to her, so it hurt her to see him like that just as much as it hurt Nita.

"He's a tough kid, he'll recover. The cops will find the bastards who did this." Robert was trying to hold back tears.

Nita couldn't believe any of this was happening. First Max, now someone was trying to kill Benjamin. She knew it was a matter of time before they came after her, or her family. She wondered why whoever did this came after Benjamin first and not her? Unless they wanted to get to her by hurting everyone she knew first, before finally taking her out. All of this was happening because she found drugs in Adrian's room, and wouldn't let it go. Susan and Roy told them that the police had already questioned them. They were waiting for Benjamin to regain consciousness before they came back up to the hospital to question him.

"We can stay if you want," Latisha told Nita.

Nita shook her head as if it was an option. There was no way she was leaving his side after this. Besides, if someone was after her, it was best she stayed there for a while. They must've sat at the hospital for two more hours before Benjamin finally woke up.

"Mom." He slowly opened his eyes. "Everyone's here." He glanced around the room and noticed Nita, her parents, and his dad. All of them rushed closer, happy to see him finally conscious.

"The police will be here soon, to talk to you," Susan said to him.

"Why? I don't know who did this." He looked at Nita. "Nita, I'm so glad you're here."

"You know I wouldn't leave your side." She smiled at him. "I'm so glad you're not dead!"

"It'll take a lot more than a few punches to kill me," Benjamin said jokingly, as he groaned from the pain of trying to sit up.

But he was right. Whoever did this, could have easily stabbed or shot him if they wanted him dead. So why bother beating him up. Unless they didn't want to kill him, but just hurt him, to send a message. Susan had stepped out to make a phone call, letting the police know Benjamin was up and able to speak with them.

"Detective Jackson will be here soon," Susan said, coming back into the room.

The last thing Nita wanted was to see the detective again. She told Benjamin that she would be back later, once the police left. She kissed him on the forehead and asked her parents to take her home.

During the car ride home, Nita didn't even need to figure out who got Benjamin beaten up. She knew it had to be Chin. After the text message she got at school warning her to leave the situation alone, she hadn't done anything that she felt would cause Benjamin's attack. She then thought back to her trip to the police station. Benjamin's attackers had to have been watching him catch him when they did. Which meant that she was most likely being watched too. Someone probably saw her going into the station. If so, this was all worse than she thought. Nita knew she couldn't just wait around to see who would be or if she would be next. She had to go back to see Chin. She needed to know what she could do to ensure that no one else would get hurt. Her parents pulled into the driveway, and as Nita got out of the car, she told her parents to go ahead inside, as she needed a minute to clear her head. As Robert and Latisha went inside, Deon was walking out of his house. He walked down from his porch, over to Nita.

"Hey, sorry to hear about Ben." He said with a sympathetic voice.

"Thanks," Nita mumbled. She began to walk inside when he stopped her.

"Nita, look, I know we ended on bad terms but..."

Nita cut him off before he could finish his sentence. "Just, stop." She wasn't in the mood for whatever it was he was trying to do. If this was some pathetic attempt to get back on her good side for a possible second chance at a relationship, he was way out of line. Deon just stood there, looking pitiful as Nita quickly went inside. She had too much on her plate to worry about her idiot ex. She knew the next thing she had to do, was mentally, and physically prepare herself for a visit to Bakers Rd.

8
Death Wish

Nita sat in bed, half-dressed, waiting until her parents were asleep to leave. It was a little after eleven. Her father was off from work, so he was knocked out by ten, and her mother always went to bed by nine-thirty even when she didn't have to work the next morning. Nita tip-toed towards her parent's bedroom door, placing her ear against it to listen for any sounds of them possibly still being awake. All she could hear was her father's snoring, and if the TV was off, she knew her mother was asleep. She quietly walked back to her bedroom, slipped on her sweatpants, sneakers, and grabbed her cell phone, heading downstairs.

She walked toward the right of each step, trying to avoid making any loud creaking noises as she walked down. She thought about bringing her mother's taser and pepper spray to defend herself but knew she would be searched the minute she walked into Chin's apartment, so it was useless. She didn't like the idea of going there so vulnerable and un-protected, but it wasn't worth the possibility of being shot or hurt the minute they found the items on her. Hopefully, Chin would be willing to talk and be civil, so things would go smoothly. She used her rideshare app to get a ride since it was too late to catch the bus. She waited out-side as her driver pulled up in his white SUV. Walking over to the car as fast as she could so they could pull off in a hurry.

"Hey, how ya doing tonight. Nita, right?" Her driver, a young Asian man asked.

"Yes. Hello."

"529 Bakers Rd.? Alright." He said as he pulled up his GPS. "So where are you headed tonight, a party?"

Nita was in no mood for a talkative driver. "Uh, no. I'm just going to visit a friend."

"Oh cool. You originally from Wicomino?" he asked.

Nita was already frustrated and decided to let him off nicely. "I don't really want to talk about it. Do you mind?"

He took that as a sign to be quiet, and it worked. They rode in silence until they reached the destination. Nita got out of the car, closing
the door. As her driver pulled off, a small part of her wanted to yell for
him to come back and take her home so she could crawl back into bed
and forget about all of this. But she knew that it wouldn't change anything. She needed to see Chin whether she wanted to or not. She took
a deep breath and walked up the stairs toward the buzzer. She pressed
it and in a matter of seconds, the short man answered.

"Hello."

"Hi, I'm here to see Chin."

Just like last time, there was a pause before he came back. "Come
up."

He buzzed her in and she walked inside, the light in the hallway
beaming just like the last time. Since it was dark outside, it gave the
building an even creepier appeal. She walked up to 202 and knocked.
The short man answered the door, a little shocked to see Nita again,
this time, alone.

"It's you again. Knew your voice sounded familiar." He said, looking at her with a dazed look in his eyes. Nita just put on a fake smile
and walked in as he scooted aside to let her pass.

"Arms out, just like last time." He had to search her for weapons.

Feeling her from head to toe, which was just as uncomfortable
as last time. He led her to the bedroom, where the woman was. He
opened the door, and the blonde Mexican woman sat by the window,
smoking a cigarette. It was like déjà vu. The short man closed the door,
and the woman glared at Nita. She wore a silk red robe, her hair tied up
in a bun with loose strands coming down in her face.

"You again. Where's your little friend?" She asked, puffing on the
cigarette.

Nita just stood there, not knowing if it was a good idea to come
closer. *You know exactly where he is.* Nita thought, a little angry that she
would even ask. "He's at home. It's just me."

"How many do you want this time?" The woman asked.

"Actually, I came here to talk."

The woman's eyes were glued to Nita like a Cheetah on its prey. She slowly put out her cigarette in the ashtray on the windowsill.

"I don't talk. You buy. Then you leave. That's how this works."

"But my friend, Benjamin, the one that was here with me the other day, he's in the hospital and-"

"What the hell does that have to do with me, little girl?" She began to get up a walk toward Nita.

"I... Well, one of my friends was killed. He's the one who gave me this address. Then I got a text threatening me. Then my friend Benjamin got beaten up badly and put in the hospital. I didn't know what else to do. I don't want anyone else I care about, or me getting hurt. I don't know what you want from me, but-"

Before Nita could even finish her sentence, the woman charged at her, grabbing her by her hair and twirling her around, putting Nita in a headlock. She pulled out a pistol from her thigh holster and put it up to Nita's right temple.

"Stupid girl. Just as stupid as Max, and that dead boyfriend of yours. That's why they're both dead.

Nita was starting to cry, terrified for her life. "Please don't kill me. Please. I won't go to the cops about any of this, I won't tell anyone you killed them I promise, I just want to go home!"

"Shut up." She pressed the gun harder against Nita's temple. Her fingers itching to pull the trigger with fury in her voice and a sinister look in her eyes. "What makes you think I killed them huh? What makes you think I got your little fruitcake friend beaten up? You have no idea what you've gotten yourself into *estúpido idiota!*"

Nita was balling hysterically. She knew she had made a mistake and was about to pay for it with her life.

"Max ran his mouth too much, leading you here was a bad idea, and he paid for it. Your boyfriend, on the other hand, was something else."

The woman laughed. "Adrian thought he had it all figured out. Boy was he wrong. Sucks they got taken out, they were great delivery boys."

Nita felt her heart sink. She couldn't believe it. Adrian was delivering drugs for Chin. Max too, although that wasn't as surprising to find out. With her nerves wrecked with fear and a gun to her head, this was all too much to bear.

"Chin is bigger than me. Bigger than your stupid little boyfriend, or you. If you want to live, you've got about ten seconds to get out of my house, or I will kill you. I don't ever want to see you again. You hear me?! Go!" She released Nita, pushing her forward, Nita falling to the floor.

She quickly got up and ran out of the room, still crying and heading toward the door. The short man watching her run out, not even amused by what had just happened. Nita ran out of the apartment, down the stairs and out the building door. She ran about two blocks, still crying before she stopped by an old bodega. She needed to catch her breath and find an address, so she could request a ride. She had a five-minute wait time which felt like forever with the state she was in. She just wanted to get home where it was safe.

After a few minutes of waiting, her driver showed up and she didn't waste another second before getting into the backseat. This time her driver was a young Latino man. He reminded her a little of Adrian. He had a similar hair type, and he had a nice smile, just like Adrian. Her entire ride home she thought about what the woman had told her. About Adrian delivering drugs. In the eight months, she and Adrian were together, nothing about him ever made her suspect that he would be involved in anything like that. Nita also wondered what the woman really meant about Chin being bigger than them. She made it sound like there could've possibly been someone else who killed Adrian and Max, and had Benjamin attacked. Nita prayed that this wasn't what that meant, but she had a feeling, that's exactly what this meant.

When the driver reached her house, she thanked him and walked slowly to her front door. She tried to move as quietly as possible, so she wouldn't wake her parents. When she got to her room, she got undressed and settled into bed. She still felt the pressure from the gun being held against her temple. She was so close to losing her life and felt like an idiot. She didn't even know what would happen now. If the woman would send anyone after her, or her family. Or if the woman was even the one who would. Nita didn't know what to think anymore. All she could do was bury her face into her pillow and cry, and hope that when she woke up the next morning all of this would be a dream.

9
The Truth Won't Set You Free

Nita woke up with a pounding headache. Mentally, she was still recovering from the night before. She had a dream about what happened at Chin's apartment. Only this time, the woman pulled the trigger, with blood and brain matter splattered on the wall of the bedroom, ending Nita's life. Waking up from the dream felt worse than the actual visit. She got out of bed, stumbling to the bathroom to get painkillers for her headache. Thankfully, it was finally the weekend after what felt like one of the longest weeks of her life. Since she didn't have school, she took the pills and decided to get back in bed for a little while before going up to the hospital to see Benjamin.

She slept for another hour before getting up at Nine and going downstairs to get breakfast. She made her way downstairs, where her mother was sitting in the living room watching TV. She assumed her father was still sleeping, which he usually did on Saturdays. She walked in to greet her mother, who had been watching the news.

"Good morning," Nita said with her scratchy morning voice, as she walked over to take a seat next to Latisha on the couch. After what had happened last night, and the horrible dream she had, she just wanted to cuddle up next to her mother and watch TV.

"Morning sweetie. Look at this, someone was killed over on Bakers Rd. in the middle of the night. A woman they said." Her mother, looking at the TV screen, didn't seem too surprised about the murder.

"What?" Nita asked. She grabbed the remote to turn the volume up. Something inside of her told her that she didn't even need to see the news to know who it was.

"A little after six this morning, a body was found in the dumpster, behind these apartments at 529 Bakers Rd. The victim, now identified as thirty-three-year-old Eva Gonzales-Cruz, was found with her throat slit and multiple stab wounds to the chest. There are currently no suspects, and we have no further details at this time."

Nita stared at the TV screen as the photo of the blonde Mexican woman sat in the upper right corner. It wasn't the woman's death that made her uneasy, but the fact that it had happened so soon. This also meant that Nita's suspicions were right. There had to be someone else. This person must have known that Nita was there last night, and felt the woman was a liability and had to be killed.

"So sad, such a beautiful young lady." Her mother shook her head and got up. "You hungry? I was going to wait until one of you got up before I made breakfast." She asked Nita.

Nita sat there, still staring at the TV, which was now on commercial.

"Hello! Earth to Amanita!" Her mother called out to her, waiting for an answer.

"Yeah, yeah, sure." Nita was too distracted with a million thoughts going through her head.

"Alright. I'll go and wake your father up, then after breakfast, we can head to the hospital to see Ben." Her mother walked into the kitchen to get started.

Nita, still on the couch, didn't even know how she would tell any of this to Benjamin, or if she even should. He had a right to know, but she didn't feel with his current situation, that it was a good time to bring any of this up. She also felt that he would blame her for his attack if she told him about her going to the police station, and she knew for a fact that he would be furious once she told him that she went to see Chin again, alone, and was almost killed for it. She instantly felt her headache starting to come back, rubbing her temples and hurrying upstairs to the bathroom to grab two more painkillers out of the bathroom cabinet. She swallowed them, then turned on the faucet and splashed cold water over her face.

What now?

THEY ARRIVED AT THE hospital at eleven, Nita stopped by the gift shop to get a little teddy bear with a pink heart in the center that reads "get well" in bold white letters. They walked up to the third floor where Benjamin's room was, and before they entered, Nita asked if she could have a few minutes alone with him. Her parents didn't mind. She walked in, and he was sitting up watching a re-run of The Jerry Springer show. He looked a little better than he did yesterday when she last saw him. But she could tell it would still be a while before he would fully recover.

"Hey." Nita greeted as she walked over to him, sitting in the chair next to his bed.

"Hey, girlie. Oh, is that for me? Adorable." He reached over, and Nita handed him the bear. "I'm so glad to see you. I've had enough of my parents. With my mom's constant crying and my dad's constant arguing with the nurses and staff, I'm so ready to get out of this place."

Nita was beginning to feel guilty, knowing that she was the reason he was in the hospital in the first place. "I'm sorry." She said, wishing she could do more to comfort him.

"No need to be sorry. My life sucks. It's not your fault." He said.

"I feel like it is."

"Why?"

"You know why."

Nita was getting teary-eyed as she talked to him. She knew she had to tell him about the murder but decided to hold off on telling him about the visit last night, or to the police station. He was in enough pain, and she didn't want to make it worse. "The blonde woman, from the apartment, she was found dead this morning. I and my mom saw it on the news."

Benjamin's eyes widened, he picked up the remote to mute the TV. "What? No way!"

"Shhh! I don't want my parents to hear us." Nita whispered. Benjamin leaned over closer. "They don't know who did it. She was stabbed to death. Stabbed to death, just like... he was."

"Don't even go there, Nita. Her dying had nothing to do with Adrian. She was a drug dealer. They either end up killed or locked up. Besides, if she was the one who got me beat up, I'm glad she's dead." He held his side, sighing with pain as he laid back down.

"So, they still don't know who did this," Nita asked.

When she came back up to the hospital yesterday afternoon for a little while, Benjamin had told her he spoke with the cops for about thirty minutes. Answering questions, giving them a useless description because his attackers wore masks. They said they would let him know when they got any leads. But he knew they wouldn't, and just wanted to be left alone.

"Nope. Still no suspects." He told her.

They were interrupted by a knock at the door. It was Latisha and Robert wanting to come in.

"We're good now, come in," Nita called out.

They walked in, going over to Benjamin and giving him hugs. Nita and Benjamin gave each other a look that meant they would finish talking about it later.

10
Real or Not Real

"Bye guys! Have a great night! Love you!" Nita told her parents, waving as they walked out the door, leaving to get into the car.

It was their Nineteenth wedding anniversary. Latisha wanted to cancel, feeling that it wasn't a good time to be going out and that she and Robert needed to stay home with Nita. Although Nita was a little fearful of staying home alone, she insisted that they enjoy their night and that she didn't want to be a burden. If worse came to worse, she had her mother's pepper spray and taser in the living room for protection. They finally agreed to go out, promising they would be back within two hours. She watched out from the window as her parents drove away. Instead of staying in her bedroom, she decided to stay downstairs and watch TV in the living room and keep an eye on the laundry she decided to do, to keep herself busy and her mind at ease.

She curled up on the couch and flipped through the channels to find something good to watch. Silver Bullet was on AMC, although she loved the film, it wasn't a good night to be watching a scary movie alone. She browsed through until she decided to watch reruns of SpongeBob on Nickelodeon. She went into the kitchen to make herself a cup of hot chocolate. Grabbing the cocoa mix from the cabinet above the microwave, she was startled by the loud buzzing sound of the dryer going off, causing her to jump, dropping the cocoa mix on the floor.

"Geez, Nita. Come on." She said to herself, grabbing a bunch of wet paper towels to clean up the mess.

She threw the paper towels away and walked out to the garage to get the clothes from the dryer. As she grabbed the round white bin and loaded the clean clothes in, she heard a popping sound, that sounded like something falling in the kitchen. She figured it was maybe the plastic cup she had out when she was making hot chocolate. Still, it made her a bit uneasy. She sat the clothes bin down and walked back into the kitchen. The plastic cup was still there, sitting next to the microwave.

She looked around to see what else it could've been and noticed a small puddle of dish soap on the floor. She grabbed a paper towel to clean it up. As she was wiping, she paused, looking up, and realizing the bottle was on the counter.

Nita suddenly felt fear creep up her spine, as she stared at the bottle of dish soap. She stood up slowly, and before her mind could fully process what was going on, she felt a cold presence upon her. She turned around, and there he was. A man, wearing a black face mask with nothing but his eyes exposed, and thick black gloves, standing tall in front of Nita dressed in all black. Before she could let out a scream for help, the man grabbed her by the throat, pushing her against the counter. She clawed at his strong rough hands as his grip got tighter. She then attempted to grab at his mask, pulling and scratching, anything to defend herself. She lodged her right index finger into his left eye causing him to flail her around, throwing her to the ground. She laid there, coughing and gagging from his grip as he tried to grab her. She tried to scream for help, but her voice was weak from being nearly strangled. Her reflexes reacted quickly as she was able to stand up and hold on to the counter. The man grabbed her by her hair and pulled her back toward him, clenching her throat from behind. She elbowed him in the stomach, freeing herself from his grasp and running into the living room.

"Help! Somebody, please! Help me!"

She was able to scream for help as the man ran into the living room after her, pulling out a knife from his back pocket. Nita grabbed the pepper spray from the table by the couch and got him right in the eyes, causing him to drop his knife. He groaned loudly in pain as Nita grabbed the glass flower vase from the same table and knocked him over the head with it. He fell to his knees and Nita ran for her life, racing toward her front door, and fumbling with the locks to open the door and get away as fast as she could. It was dark, as she ran straight out of her front yard, slamming right into Deon, screaming.

"Nita! Are you okay? It's me, everything's alright! What happened?" He yelled as he grabbed her shoulders trying to calm her down.

"He's in there! He tried to kill me!" Nita was sobbing hysterically.

Deon looked over at the house, with the front door still wide open. "Wait here." He said.

"No! Don't go in there!" Nita warned, grabbing at his t-shirt trying to stop him from going in.

Deon ran into the house, as Nita sat outside, still crying. Not even a minute later coming back out.

"Nobody's there." He said, walking up to Nita.

Her eyes got big with tears. "What?"

"I didn't see anyone, Nita."

"He's there! I swear!" Nita yelled. "We've got to get out of here!" She grabbed at his shirt.

"Okay, okay. Let's go to my house, and we'll call the police. He couldn't have gotten that far."

He walked a distraught Nita over to his house.

When they got there, she sat at his kitchen table, silent and horrified by what had just happened to her. First, he called the cops, then Nita's parents. Deon didn't say much to the cops, just that his neighbor was attacked by an intruder. He waited patiently with her for the cops to arrive, trying to be as comforting as he could. But nothing he could say or do could help.

TWO HOURS LATER, NITA and her parents were at the police station waiting for Detective Jackson to finish going over the night's events with Nita. Deon had told the police that he didn't see anyone in the house when he went to go check. Just a broken flower vase in the living room. The police also didn't find any signs of forced entry, fingerprints, or footprints. The knife the man had was also gone, there was no evidence of anyone being in the house. They had officers drive around the neighborhood to check for suspects, but they found no one. They also spoke with neighbors, to see if anyone saw anything suspicious around the time Nita was attacked. No one saw anything.

Detective Jackson took a seat at the desk where the Matua family was sitting. "So, you say this masked man got into your house somehow, without you hearing a thing?" She asked Nita.

"Yes. I don't know how he got in."

"Okay. You don't remember any specific features about him? Maybe his eyes, body type?" Detective Jackson asked.

"His eyes were brown. That's all." Nita had told them previously that the man was wearing all black, from head to toe. So, there wasn't much of a description she could give them.

The detective let out a sigh. "So, we don't have a face, no evidence of an intruder or any attack at all. Just a shattered vase and a witness, your neighbor Deon saying he heard you screaming. You say this man tried to strangle you, but there are no bruises, your neck looks fine."

"Are you trying to accuse my daughter of lying!" Robert shouted at the detective.

"Mr. Matua, calm down. I'm not accusing her of anything, I just want to get to the bottom of this." Detective Jackson's eyes went back to Amanita. "Are you sure you can't think of anyone who would want to hurt you?"

"No."

Nita wasn't ready to tell any of them about Chin, Max, or Adrian's drugs. Whoever attacked her, had it planned out well. Well enough to not leave any evidence behind, which is why he was trying to strangle her. He only grabbed his knife as a last resort, to get the job done. "But he was there, I swear. You've got to believe me." Nita said with urgency.

"Look, I'm giving you the benefit of doubt because of what happened to your friend Benjamin. But there is nothing we can do with no leads or evidence. I'm sorry." Detective Jackson said.

"So, what now? We just wait around for this person to attack my daughter again? How do we know he won't come back?" Latisha was worried and frustrated.

"If you need anything, give me a call. I'll look more into this, see what I can come up with, but I can't make any promises." Said, Detective Jackson. "Just keep your doors and windows secure. I'll have a car patrolling the area tonight. Amanita, I wouldn't recommend you being home alone for a while."

Nita just shook her head, agreeing.

"You three have a good night, and call me if you need anything, I mean it." Detective Jackson got up from her chair and walked them to the door.

When they got home, Latisha and Robert decided to stay downstairs for the night. Nita didn't want to be alone and decided to join them, making a bed with blankets and pillows, sleeping in the living room with them. Robert told them that first thing tomorrow morning he was getting all the locks changed, even installing new latches on the windows. The cops may not have believed Nita's story, but Robert would make sure his family was safe by any means necessary. Her parents fell asleep eventually, but Nita couldn't sleep at all. All she could think about was her attack. The blonde woman was dead, Ben was in the hospital and now someone was after her and no one other than her parents seemed to believe her. It was bad enough that everyone already thought she was crazy and a liar. She felt stuck, at a dead end. Max and the blonde woman were her only links to any of this mess. There was the short man from the apartment, but she was sure he was M.I.A. by now, if not dead. Nita was in a world of trouble and had no way of getting out.

11

Betrayal

It was Monday morning, Nita slipped on her dark blue denim jeans, looking at herself in the mirror in her bedroom. Her parents wanted her to stay home, but after spending all of Sunday cooped up in the room, not answering Benjamin's calls or eating all day, she wanted to get out of the house. Even if it meant being at school. Going to school would be tough without Benjamin, but she figured there was nothing anyone could say or do to make her feel any worse than she already did. All anyone seemed to do was stare anyway, and after she beat up Carla, anyone would be a fool to challenge her. After getting fully dressed, and brushing her hair, she heard a soft knock on her door.

"Yeah?" Nita answered. In walked her mother.

"Hey, honey. Just checking on you." She walked in, closing the door slightly. "I also wanted to let you know that I made an appointment for you to see the therapist tomorrow."

Nita sighed deeply. "That's fine, I guess."

"It's just one appointment. We'll see how it goes. This doesn't mean that you have to keep going."

"I know," Nita said softly, still brushing her hair in the same spot, staring at her reflection in the mirror with dead eyes not even glancing at her mother once.

Her mother walked over to her, taking the brush from her hand and sitting it on the bed.

"I don't want you to think your father and I don't believe you, we do. We're just worried."

"I understand, mom."

"Okay." Latisha kissed her daughter on the cheek. "Well, I'm on my way out. Your father will be ready to take you to school in a few. Love you."

Nita hesitated before acknowledging her mother. "Love you too."

Latisha stood at the doorway, still looking at her daughter. "Just try and keep it together today, okay?" She walked out, closing the door behind her.

Nita knew her parents were worried, but the last thing she wanted to do was go back to therapy. Sitting in that cold room talking about her problems which never seemed to lead to any real answers. She knew she still couldn't bring up any details about the drugs, and the murders. She could, her therapist was very strict about patient confidentiality. Nita just didn't feel comfortable discussing too much.

Robert dropped Nita off at school, making sure she didn't want to change her mind and go back home before she got out of the car. She assured him over and over that it was fine, and she would call him and leave early if she needed too. As she walked inside the school building, the stares began. A few whispers followed by a few discreet, mean laughs. As she walked toward her locker, she saw Ms. Stone in her classroom, sitting at her desk. Then suddenly remembered about the group therapy, where Ms. Stone had revealed Nita's suicide attempt to everyone. With everything that had gone on the past few days, Nita had forgotten about it. She continued walking past, dreading going to English, and having to look her in the eyes. As she was getting her books for the first period, Mr. Nelson had approached her locker.

"Amanita, good morning." He greeted.

"Oh, hi Mr. Nelson." Nita could tell by his constant adjusting of his tie, that something was off about him.

"Do you mind if we speak for a second? It's important." He asked.

"Yeah, sure."

"Follow me." He walked her to his classroom, where a few students were already seated, waiting for class to begin. "Would you guys mind stepping outside for a minute? I need to speak with my student in private."

The two girls and the boy sitting on opposite sides of the classroom didn't say a word, just got up and walked out, giving Nita shady looks as they passed by. When they were out, Mr. Nelson closed the door and asked Nita to take a seat. She sat in one of the front row seats, sitting her books on the desk in front of her.

"From what I know, you were at Ms. Stone's group therapy last week." He asked, taking a seat next to her at another desk.

"Yes." Nita broke eye contact, feeling glum with a reminder of what happened.

"I was told that she revealed some very personal information about you. Something she had no business doing, and I just wanted to apologize on her behalf."

"Shouldn't she be the one apologizing?"

Mr. Nelson pressed his lips together nervously. "Yeah, about that. She only knew about what happened to you because I told her."

Nita's eyes were frozen on him, in shock. "What? How?"

"My sister works at the animal hospital, with your mother. The day after your suicide attempt, your mother was an emotional mess. She was crying, venting to one of her friends about what happened. My sister overheard everything." He sighed heavily. "She knew that you were one of my students and told me about it. I told Ms. Stone, but it wasn't my intention to be a gossip. We were genuinely worried about you. I'm sorry, Amanita."

She couldn't believe it. She didn't know who to be more upset with. Her mother for telling someone about it when she was the main one wanting to keep it a secret, the gossiping hag who decided to run her mouth to a faculty member of the school, or Mr. Nelson for even repeating what he had heard. Nita wasn't even upset with Ms. Stone anymore.

"Ms. Stone was only trying to help. Although I don't agree with it, you must know that her intentions weren't to be malicious." Mr. Nelson said.

Nita had heard enough and just wanted the conversation to be over. "It's alright. I'm over it." Nita grabbed her books and got up. "I'm going to get to class. I'll see you later. Thanks for apologizing."

"Of course, Ms. Matua." He smiled back as she left the classroom.

As she walked down the hall, she saw Carla going into the restroom, her nose still badly bruised from their fight. Although they weren't friends, she felt bad for Carla. Nita was so wrapped up in her problems, she didn't think about the fact that others lost Adrian too. His parents, friends, even Carla. They were together for three years before he and Nita started dating. His death must've taken its toll on Carla as well. If it were the other way around, Nita felt that she would probably be treating Carla the same way out of hurt and anger. She walked toward the restroom, going in after her. She walked in and could tell that Carla was in the handicap stall at the end. Nita wanted to apologize for the fight. She walked inside the stall that was right next to Carla's and sat down. That's when she heard Carla crying quietly.

"Carla?" Nita asked in a whisper.

She must have startled Carla, who probably wasn't paying attention to anyone else coming in. "Who is that?" She yelled.

"It's me, Nita. Are you okay?"

"What do you care!" Carla said angrily, sniffling.

"I just... wanted to apologize for the other day. Breaking your nose and stuff. Sorry about that."

Carla didn't respond, but Nita could still hear her crying and sniffling in the other stall. Nita was beginning to feel like this was a mistake. She got up, leaving the stall and walking toward the door when Carla responded.

"You think you knew him, you didn't." She said from the stall.

Nita stopped, turning around. "Excuse me?" She responded in a defensive tone.

Carla began to walk out of the stall. "I know you loved him, but, Adrian was, Adrian."

"What's that supposed to mean?"

"I wasn't lying. When I told you that I was with him that night."

Nita remembered Carla telling her that she was with Adrian the night of his basketball game.

"Look, I came in here to apologize for ruining your face, not to start more drama." Nita began to walk out again.

"I'm not telling you this to start drama, I'm telling you this because you deserve to know."

Nita stopped and turned around again. Carla walked closer to her. "That night, Adrian and I, we slept together," Carla admitted.

Nita was pissed, she wanted to punch Carla in the face again and storm out, but something told her to so stay, be calm and hear her out.

"Afterwards, he felt guilty, and told me it didn't mean anything, and that he loved you." Carla continued. "It hurt so much. To make things worse, I got pregnant. He died before I could tell him. I got rid of it two days after Adrian's funeral."

Nita was stunned. She didn't know how to react, or if she should even believe Carla.

"Remember when he ditched you after the game, then you couldn't get in touch with him the whole day after?" Carla asked. "He wasn't answering your calls or texts. Remember he told you that he wasn't feeling well because he got too drunk? Well, now you know why."

Carla pulled a paper from her purse. It was an ultrasound. Dated eight weeks after the night Carla was referring to. This wasn't proof that she was telling the truth, but Nita knew Carla had it bad for Adrian, and she would've jumped at any chance to be with him again. Adrian was a sweetheart, but he was still an attractive teenage boy, with more popularity than he could handle at times. Nita didn't want to believe that Adrian would cheat on her, but thinking back to that night, it wasn't exactly hard to believe.

"I'm sorry." Carla looked devastated. "If it means anything, he did love you."

Nita placed her hand on Carla's shoulder. "I'm sorry about your baby Carla." Nita didn't say another word. She just left.

She didn't even bother going to the first period. Instead, she went out to the football field to sit on the bleachers. She needed to be alone, to deal with the overload of information she had to take in. It seemed like from the moment she found the drugs in Adrian's room, everything she thought she knew, was a lie. She felt betrayed by those she thought she could trust, her teacher, her boyfriend, even her mother. She couldn't do anything but cry.

After the first period had let out, Nita climbed down from the bleachers, contemplating calling her dad to come to pick her up. She didn't think that she could finish the rest of the school day. She walked around the side of the building, where she ran into Ms. Stone, who was taking a smoke break. She wanted to avoid her, but Ms. Stone saw her before she could turn around.

"Amanita!" She called out to her. Nita stopped. "Hey, I know Mr. Nelson talked with you already, and I know how you must be feeling. I'm truly sorry about what I did. I feel awful."

"It's okay. I know you didn't mean any harm."

Ms. Stone dropped her cigarette, crushing it with her left heel. "Let me make it up to you. I'll take you to Alberto's for pizza after school."

"Umm, that sounds nice but maybe another time. I'm going home early; my dad is on his way." Nita pulled out her phone and began to text her father.

Ms. Stone looked a little disappointed but playfully brushed it off. "No problem! I'll take a rain check." She said smiling. "I gotta get to class. See you tomorrow?"

"Yeah," Nita replied.

Ms. Stone quickly pranced back inside, and Nita continued toward the front of the building to wait for her father. He must've been sleeping because it took him longer than usual to reply.

She waited out front for him for about ten minutes, when she saw Mr. Nelson walking toward his car. Odd thing was, he was getting in on the passenger's side. It wasn't his car, but someone else's. Nita looked closer and noticed that there was another gentleman on the driver's side. They sat in the car for about a minute before Mr. Nelson got out. Nita hid behind a nearby bush to avoid being seen. She watched Mr. Nelson walk back into the school building. His face looked agitated like he just had a very uncomfortable conversation or gotten bad news. He was trying to remain nonchalant as he walked back inside, but Nita knew there was nothing nonchalant about what went on in that car. After Mr. Nelson was back inside, Nita came from behind the bush just when the car was pulling off, getting a look at the driver. Her jaw dropped, and her stomach felt like acid was about to burn through it. It was the short man, from Chin's apartment.

12
Set Me Free

"Benjamin, say something." Said Nita as she sat next to his hospital bed.

Her father had taken her up to the hospital to see him a little after he had picked her up from school. She had finally told him everything. About going to the police station, visiting Chin and almost getting herself killed. The attack on Saturday night. Then she told him about what she had heard and seen at school that day. Carla telling her about the baby, and Adrian cheating, also Mr. Nelson getting out of a car, where she saw the man from Chin's apartment. Benjamin just laid there, quiet. Nita didn't know if this meant that he was mad at her, or shocked, or scared. After a minute of silence, he finally replied.

"Are you sure it was him?" Benjamin asked.

"Yes. I know his face. I know it was him, for sure."

"So, this means that Mr. Nelson knows him. That could mean anything."

Nita gave him a serious stare. "Ben, it can't be a coincidence."

"Why can't it be?"

"It just can't be."

"Nita, you need to relax. All of this is really getting to you and it's not healthy. Especially after your attack. Still can't believe that happened. I should've been there to protect you."

Nita bent over, covering her face with her hands. "This is too much." She said, feeling overwhelmed. "I just feel like I can't catch a break."

"Look, don't worry about it. Even if they know each other, so what? Wicomino County isn't that big."

"I guess." Nita sat back, with her arms crossed.

"So, about Carla..." Benjamin began to ask. Nita rolled her eyes. "You really think she was telling the truth? Not about the baby obviously, but about it being Adrian's? I mean, I never liked the guy, so it wouldn't surprise me that he was a cheating bastard."

"It doesn't matter now anyway."

"Of course, it matters! You've been running around playing detective ever since you found those drugs in his room. You've almost got yourself killed, twice! I could've been killed! All for what? Some douchebag jock that was cheating on you anyway!" Benjamin was upset because he was right. "I told you the minute you found the rippers to let it go."

"I know! I don't need you to remind me!" Now Nita was mad. "Even if he did make a mistake and slept with Carla, that doesn't mean that he deserved to die, and I sure as hell didn't deserve to walk in and find him like that! What about me? What about what I went through? Half the town still thinks I'm a murderer!"

They were interrupted by the nurse, who was coming in to do her rounds. "How are you feeling mister?" She asked, trying not to make things awkward after walking in on their argument.

"I'm fine," Benjamin answered. The nurse was getting ready to change his bedding, so Nita felt that it would be a good time to leave.

"I should be getting home." She got up from the chair. "I'll text you later."

She gave him a kiss on his forehead and left his room to go meet her father downstairs. She didn't mean for her visit to turn into an argument, but she felt like Benjamin wasn't seeing things from her perspective. It wasn't just about Adrian anymore. It was never just about him, to begin with. Nita's life was turned upside down after he was killed. Finding the killer didn't just mean getting justice for Adrian, but also clearing her own name. Then maybe, she could have a normal life again. The fact that her best friend couldn't see that, is what made her upset. Besides her parents, Benjamin knew her better than anyone.

"AMANITA, ARE YOU READY?" Her mother yelled for the second time from the bottom of the stairs.

Nita was tying her shoelaces, taking her time getting dressed. It was Tuesday morning, and she was in no rush to get to her therapy appointment.

"Be downstairs in five minutes please!" Her mother yelled again.

"Okay," Nita mumbled to herself.

She wasn't trying to be a pain on purpose, but she really wasn't looking forward to going. She was also still a little upset over her mother confiding in a friend about her suicide attempt. She decided not to bring it up, and forgive her, but it didn't mean that Nita wasn't still hurt because of it. She grabbed her cell phone and slowly made her way downstairs. Latisha was clearing out the dishes from the sink, while Robert sat and read the morning paper.

"Finally." Her mother said.

Nita rolled her eyes. "Your father has a meeting at the firehouse, so it's just me and you today." She said, smiling at Nita. Latisha had taken the day off from work, so she could take Nita to her appointment. After putting all the dishes in the dishwasher, she grabbed her car keys and kissed Robert goodbye. Nita, walking into the kitchen did the same.

"Have a good day today baby girl." Her father told her.

"I will dad."

Latisha and Nita headed out the door, getting into the car. Nita fastened her seatbelt while her mother got in on the driver's side.

"You ready?" Her mother asked with an enthusiastic tone.

"To conquer the day? Sure." Nita replied.

Twenty minutes later they arrived at the Braxton Grove Wellness center. Nita started seeing Dr. Tanya Braxton a week after Adrian's death. During the first visit, Nita didn't even speak. She saw Dr. Braxton three times a week for three months. At first, she wasn't sure if Nita would ever recover from the events surrounding Adrian's death, but she never gave up on her. Nita told her everything, from her relationship with Deon, the day she met Adrian, and the day they started dating to the night she lost her virginity. Nita didn't end her therapy sessions because she didn't like Dr. Braxton, she ended them because she wanted to gain her independence back. Ending therapy and getting back in school was a huge stepping stone for Nita's return to a normal life, although nothing had been normal since.

When they walked in, the receptionist, someone new that they didn't recognize greeted them immediately.

"Good morning! Are you here to see Dr. Braxton or Dr. Grove?" The bubbly blonde woman asked.

"Dr. Braxton. We're not new, my daughter is an ex-patient of hers." Latisha replied.

"Okay great! Just sign in, and I'll let her know you're here!" The woman grabbed a clipboard and placed it on the counter.

"Thanks," Latisha said, grabbing the clipboard and handing it to Nita.

She put her name and arrival time on the paper, handing it back to the receptionist, and they took a seat in the empty waiting room. There was no television, just a radio with smooth jazz playing, and the walls were covered in paintings of Hydrangeas and blue Irises. Nita used to think the paintings were loud and distracting. Dr. Braxton told her that the Hydrangea's represented emotions, and express gratitude for being understood, while the blue Irises represented faith and hope. This type of attention to beauty and understanding of life and nature is one of the reasons Nita admired her so much.

A few minutes later, the door leading to the back opened, and Dr. Braxton appeared with a smile. "Amanita, I'm ready for you now."

Nita got up from her seat, her mother waving to Dr. Braxton, who waved back at her. She walked through the door, immediately giving Dr. Braxton a hug. "I'm glad you came back to see me Amanita." She said, hugging her back.

They went into her office, which was naked with a nude-colored interior. No paintings or pictures on the walls. Unlike the waiting room, she wanted her patients to focus on just her during their sessions. Nita took a seat on the cream-colored love seat, while Dr. Braxton took a seat in her white metal chair, facing Nita.

"So, what brings you here today?" Dr. Braxton asked, crossing her legs and placing her hands on her lap. "Your appointment was listed as an emergency, which is why you got an appointment at such short notice."

"You know, stuff," Nita said, playfully.

"You're still having the nightmares, aren't you?"

Nita wasn't there to discuss those but felt it was necessary, to be honest anyway. "I am, yes. But that's not why I'm here."

"Oh?" Dr. Braxton was intrigued.

Nita had no idea where to start. She sat closer to the edge of the love seat. "I was attacked this past weekend."

Dr. Braxton's jaw dropped. "Oh, my goodness, Amanita what happened?"

"Someone broke into my home on Saturday night. Tried to kill me, but I got away. My best friend Ben was beaten up a few days ago, so things haven't been too good."

"Did they catch those responsible?"

"No, not yet. Both times the attackers wore masks."

Dr. Braxton walked over to grab her notepad while Nita spoke. "You have no idea who could have done this?" she asked, jotting down notes.

Nita really wanted to tell her everything, but her gut wouldn't allow it. "No." She started to get teary-eyed. "It sucks because my attacker left no evidence, so everyone thinks I'm a liar."

Dr. Braxton walked up and handed her a handkerchief she kept in her blouse pocket. "What do your parents think?"

"They believe me, I guess."

"I'm sure they do, they have no reason not to. You're their child, and they love you... So, how is your friend doing after his attack?"

"He's fine now."

"Have you been able to sleep since?"

"Yes, but hardly."

"You say you're still having bad dreams, describe your nightmares to me."

Nita went into detail, describing every nightmare she had since the day she went back to school until last night. Dr. Braxton took notes as she listened.

"Seems like there is a pattern here. In most of these dreams, your deceased boyfriend is trying to harm you. It could be the guilt you still feel for his unsolved murder, which is normal."

Dr. Braxton stopped writing and sat her notepad down on the floor.

"I want to talk more about the dream with the blood on the walls. You had this dream right before Ben's attack, right?"

"Yes," Nita replied softly.

"Seems to me, that it was your conscious telling you that you had blood on your hands. Do you feel responsible for your friend's attack, Amanita?"

Nita started to get a sour feeling in the pit of her stomach. Dr. Braxton was spot on and didn't even know it. Nita did in fact feel responsible for what happened to Benjamin.

"Maybe," Nita said.

"Why would you feel responsible? Did you do something wrong?"

Nita took a deep breath and admitted the truth. "Yes."

Dr. Braxton's eyes lit up with curiosity. "Would you like to share?" She asked.

"I took something, that I had no business taking. It got my friend and I involved in a bad situation with a bad person."

Dr. Braxton could tell that Nita didn't want to reveal too much, so she backed off a little. "Okay. Do you think this bad person attacked you in your home on Saturday?"

"No. They... left town before it happened. I won't have to worry about them anymore. But I think that person has a friend, who is still upset over the situation."

"Maybe you can try getting in contact with this friend to clear things up?"

"Maybe." Nita leaned in closer. "Can I ask you a question?" She asked.

"Sure."

Nita thought about Adrian, and what Carla told her. "Have you ever felt like you don't really know people like you thought you did?"

"Oh yes. I can relate to that."

"How did you deal with it?"

"If it's something I can't change, I try my best to let it go."

Nita also remembered seeing her teacher with the short man from the apartment. "I wish it were that easy."

"It isn't, I know. But there isn't much you can do to change people. If they're important to you, maybe you can approach them about it. Let them know how you feel and see where it goes."

Nita was getting tired and ready to go. "Thanks for seeing me today." She got up from the love seat.

"Of course. You still have twenty minutes, anything else you want to talk about before you go?"

"No. I think I'm okay."

Dr. Braxton got up from her chair and walked Nita back out to the waiting room. "Call me if you need anything, I'm always here." She smiled at Nita before escorting her out.

"I know." Nita smiled, giving her a hug before leaving. Her mother, still sitting in the waiting room, got up from the chair.

"Done already?" She asked.

"Yeah." Said, Nita.

Once they got into the car, Latisha asked how it went. "Good. I'm glad I came." Nita told her.

"I'm happy to hear that sweetie." She kissed her daughter on the forehead., then pulled out of the parking lot.

During the drive home, Nita thought about what Dr. Braxton said about letting things go. If what Carla said about Adrian was true, there was no sense in letting it get to her anymore, because Adrian wasn't around to tell his side, and there was nothing she could do about it now. As for Mr. Nelson, she thought about possibly asking him about the car situation, just to see how he knew the man at least. She didn't want to think about the other possibility, that maybe, Mr. Nelson was involved with drugs.

13

Who You Really Are

Nita sat in Chemistry class yawning and feeling weary, in the far-left corner towards the back. She hadn't gotten much sleep since Saturday night, and the stress from her attack still lingered. Mr. Nelson was giving a lecture on molecular formulas. As he walked back and forth, reading each slide on the projector, Nita couldn't help but stare. All she kept thinking about was seeing him in the car with that man. All night after her session with Dr. Braxton, she kept thinking about it. She wanted to just go up and ask him point-blank, "How do you know him?" but she knew that was impossible. She thought about Benjamin being right, that maybe it wasn't anything to stress over. He could've been a relative or a friend without any connection to drugs at all. It wouldn't sound too hard to believe if the car situation hadn't looked so sketchy. She then randomly remembered the day of the fight she had with Carla. Mr. Nelson pulled her into his classroom to talk, and right before their conversation ended, he got that strange phone call that seemed to make him upset.

Strange phone calls and visits in the middle of the school day that make you uneasy? "No, that's not suspicious at all." That last part, Nita hadn't realized she said out loud sarcastically. Luckily not loud enough for anyone to understand, but loud enough to catch Mr. Nelson's attention.

"Amanita, can you tell me the molecular formula for high fructose corn syrup?" Mr. Nelson asked.

His question caught her off guard. "Huh?" She replied, confused.

"Molecular formula... high fructose corn syrup... please?"

The entire class suddenly had all eyes on her. She hated being put on the spot and knew her not paying attention was the only reason he called on her.

"Umm... C6H12O6." Nita remembered from a previous lesson. Science was one of her top subjects, so her quick comeback was no surprise to him.

"Good. Glad to see you were paying attention." He said to her, with a slight smirk. He was teasing obviously, Nita knew that and decided to join in.

"Of course. You are my favorite teacher, after all."

"Why thank you, Amanita."

A few of her classmates rolled their eyes as Mr. Nelson immediately went back to his lesson. He really was her favorite teacher, which made all of this so much more unsettling. She didn't want to think anything negative about him after seeing him with the short man but couldn't help it. She had decided not to bring it up to him. It wasn't her place to anyway, even if she knew what to say. A part of her really wanted to let all of this go, but another part of her knew that she couldn't. There was no way of telling if her, her parent's or Benjamin's life was still in jeopardy. Nita hated feeling so helpless. She felt like a sitting duck, with no one to turn to for any real help. Going back to therapy was refreshing, but it didn't exactly fix her problems.

Class dismissed, Nita grabbed her books and headed toward her locker. She passed Max's old locker, which still had notes, drawings, and dead flowers taped to it. Left by the few friends he had. Nita stood there, she still felt guilty about his death, and it filled her with torment. She knew that if anyone could help right now, it probably would've been him. The blonde woman told her that he was a delivery boy with Adrian. This meant that he worked for Chin, the person who had it out for her. Her eyes gazed at his locker as she thought about what was in it. If the stuff left by his friends were still there, then that meant that his locker hadn't been cleaned out yet. She wondered if there could be anything inside that could give her clues to Chin's real identity. If she was going to attempt a break-in, she would have to come back when school let out. Wednesdays, Thursdays, and Fridays are when most after school clubs took place, so she knew that the doors would be open. She just needed a quick way to get in and out without getting caught.

Three o'clock rolled around, and Nita sat on the bleachers, waiting for the school to clear out after the bell rang. Most of the students were gone by two-thirty, with some lingering around to socialize. By three, the school was cleared out with the only students left being ones involved in after school activities. Most teachers didn't leave until about three-thirty, but most of them spent their time cooped up in their classroom getting paperwork done. She decided to sit for a little while longer, playing a game on her phone to pass the time. Three-forty-five rolled around, and it looked as if the school was mostly empty. It seemed like a good time to go for it. She climbed down from the bleachers and walked back toward the school building. Going through the back door, the halls were dead empty. She walked past the classrooms, most being empty with a teacher or two still at their desk. She made her way up to the second floor where Max's locker was. She peeked into nearby classrooms to see if they were empty. To her surprise, they all were. She walked up to his locker, eyeing the lock. When Nita was thirteen, she had gotten her diary stolen by girls that had been bullying her in gym class. After school, Benjamin had snuck into the girl's locker room with her and showed her how to break open the lock, getting her diary back. She had an impressive memory, so it's something she never forgot.

She grabbed the lock, shimming it using an aluminum soda can she had in her purse. She inserted the shim into the space between the padlock body and the shackle, on the opposite side of the shackle's locking grove. Once it was in, she turned the shim while working the shackle upwards, then downwards. The shackle pulled the shim into the locking mechanism as it was being turned. Within a minute, the lock was opened. She opened the locker, finding nothing but old journals from different subjects, junk food wrappers, and a math textbook. She picked up the journals, flipping through them. Most of it was scribbled notes with random drawings of anime characters. Nita was beginning to regret her decision to do this, taking quick glances to make sure no one was coming. She picked up one of the journals which were a green composition book. It was labeled "Chemistry Class/Mr. Nelson" Flipping through it, she came across a page with formulas written on it. It looked like regular class notes, but something stood out.

C9H13N

This formula didn't look familiar, and Nita was too good in science to not know what it was. There was also something else odd about how it was written. The letters, C, H, and N were written with force. Like he had gone over them with the pen a bunch of times. Nita looked closer.

C...H...N?

That's when it hit her. "CHIN!"

She clasped her right hand over her mouth as the name slipped out. The formula was unfamiliar because it was a drug formula. There was no way, Nita knew she was officially losing her mind.

"Amanita Matua! What are you doing at a deceased student's locker after school hours?" Principal Morris was walking down the hall, startling Nita as she fumbled to quickly stuff the journal in her purse. She didn't immediately respond, figuring she was in deep trouble anyway and it didn't matter what she said.

"I... umm." She stumbled over here words.

"You what?" he asked, getting closer.

"I... I was just looking for something." She looked at him nervously as he stared at her, not seeming convinced.

"Well whatever it was, I hope you found it. I could suspend you for this, you know that."

Nita didn't say anything. She felt ashamed and was prepared to take whatever punishment was about to follow.

"But... considering your recent mental troubles, I'm going to let you off the hook this one time."

Nita was shocked but relieved. Still silent. "I heard about what happened to you over the weekend. I'm sorry." As sympathetic as he was being, his strict tone of voice hadn't changed at all.

"Get out of here young lady."

Nita didn't even think twice, she swiftly closed the locker and ran down the hallway. Bolting down the steps and toward the front of the building. She texted her dad to tell him she was ready. Before school ended she had told him she would be staying after to get some extra credit work done since he was picking her up from school all week, so she wouldn't have to walk alone. He couldn't get there fast enough. While waiting, she opened the journal, flipping back to the page with the formula on it. She pulled up the internet on her phone and typed the letters and numbers into the search engine. Her body already knew, but she had to be sure.

AMPHETAMINE.

It all made sense now. Those letters were written to spell out Chin on purpose. In Mr. Nelson's class. There was no way any of this was a coincidence anymore. The odd phone call, the short man, Chin having Nita's phone number and knowing where she and Benjamin lived. The clever connection with the name was like the cherry on top of the cake. He was Chin. Mr. Nelson was Chin. He had to be.

14
A Plan

When Nita got home, she waited for her mother to arrive from work, so she could take Nita to see Benjamin. Nita had to show him what she found. He was in denial and had to see for himself. When she arrived at the hospital, she told her mother she wanted some alone time with Benjamin. After chatting with him for a few minutes, her mother left to go to the cafeteria, giving them privacy. Nita showed him the formula, and how it was written in the journal. She pulled up the formula on her search engine and showed him that it was for rippers. She explained that none of this could be a coincidence. Benjamin was overwhelmed with this information. He flipped through the journal, listening to Nita, not sure what to believe.

"This is wild, man." He said, shaking his head, with the journal on his lap.

"What do we do now? I can't go to the police with a journal full of scribble accusing my teacher of being some drug lord and killing three people." Nita said anxiously.

"Whoa... who said anything about going to the police? Sure, this is some serious stuff, but it's hardly proof."

"Benjamin!"

"What Nita? This being in a journal for Mr. Nelson's class is odd, but it's not proof that he's Chin. Although, the name thing really is clever."

"How can you still be so skeptic after everything I've told you?" Nita was getting frustrated.

"I'm not saying I don't believe you... I just... I just don't know what to think anymore."

"I know it's a lot. How do you think I feel? I would've never in a million years thought Mr. Nelson could be capable of anything like this. How are we supposed to go back to school after this? There is no way I can even look at him after seeing all this."

Nita got up from the chair and paced the room. Benjamin sat the book down on the chair by the bed where she was sitting. He pulled the covers off him and moved his legs to the right, trying to get up. He hissed in pain from his badly bruised ribs that weren't healed yet. He tried to walk over to the little dresser drawer where his clothes were from the night he came in. Nita saw him struggling and went over to help.

"Ben, you know you shouldn't be up like this." She said, gently holding his side, guiding him back to the bed. "You should lie back down." But he refused.

"Nita, listen to me. If you really think Mr. Nelson is behind all of this, you need to find real proof before it's too late."

Nita sat back down, picking up the journal and placing it back inside her bag. "Tomorrow is Thursday, Ms. Stone has book club after school, right?"

"Yeah."

"Could you grab my jeans for me?" He asked.

Nita walked over to the dresser drawer, opened it, and grabbed them. "Look in the right pocket."

She was confused by his request but dug into the pocket and inside was a little bag. She pulled it out, and it contained two pills, rippers. Her eyes lit up with disbelief.

"What are you doing with these! Are these the pills from Adrian's room? Or the ones you bought when we went to the apartment? Why do you still have these!?" She demanded the truth from him.

"It's not what you think. The pills from the apartment, I flushed those the same day. I didn't get rid of the ones from Adrian's room immediately just in case. The night I was attacked, I was going to flush them, but got distracted from my dad yelling for me to take the garbage out. I stuffed them in my pocket to flush when I came back inside, but, as you can see I never got that chance."

Nita didn't know what to say. She just stood there with the pills in her hand. "Well, what do you want with them now?"

"I want you to stay after the book club tomorrow. Too much student traffic in and out of classrooms for you to do this during the school day without being seen. When you get a chance, go to Mr. Nelson's classroom. The door will be unlocked, they always are. Plant the pills. I'll call the cops with an anonymous tip about the drugs in the morning."

"Benjamin, I can't do that!" She protested.

"You're so sure it's him, right? Then it should be easy."

Nita suddenly felt the guilt of her accusations. Finding proof was one thing, but planting proof was on a whole other level.

"I don't know."

"Either you do it, or I do it when I get out of here. If you're not dead by then."

Nita was a little hurt by his blunt words. But he was serious. He would have no issue doing this, and she knew it. Besides, he had a point. The longer it took to find the person behind this, the more her life and the lives of those she cared about was in jeopardy.

"I'll do it." She said, with a guilt-ridden voice.

"Worse case, if it isn't him, he'll just lose his job. But this is California, he could always get another teaching gig in the slums of LA. But at least he won't be in prison." Benjamin said.

This made Nita feel even worse than she already did. But if this was a chance to catch Chin, it was worth the risk. They were interrupted by Latisha knocking slightly before entering.

"Hey honey, you ready to go?" She asked Nita.

"Yeah." She gave Ben his usual goodbye kiss on the forehead and told him she'd text him when she got home.

"Nurse says you're doing a little better. That's great to hear." Latisha said to Benjamin.

"Yeah, pretty soon I'll leave this hell hole to go back to my other one. At least my other one has junk food though."

Latisha and Nita giggled at his humor.

"Bye Ben." Said Latisha, as they left the room.

"Bye guys."

Nita hated seeing him in the hospital. She couldn't wait for him to get better, so she could have him around again. If Mr. Nelson really was Chin, then this would all be over soon, and Nita should've felt a sense of relief. But all she felt since the moment She found the journal, was fear.

That night, Nita was awake in bed, struggling to sleep. All she could think about was this plan to plant the drugs. Not only that, but having to sit through his class tomorrow, and having to look him in the face. A man who she admired and trusted. A man who possibly killed Adrian, and Max, and the blonde woman from the apartment, or had them killed. A drug dealer, and a murderer.

15
I've Got You Now

That morning, Nita felt like she was going to vomit the entire time she sat in Mr. Nelson's class. She couldn't focus, she was scared and felt intimidated by his presence. She laid her head down on her desk, her long hair draped over her arms. Mr. Nelson noticed that she looked unwell and walked over toward her desk.

"Amanita, are you feeling alright?" He asked, placing his arm on her shoulder.

This startled Nita, causing her to jump out of fear, her hair flailing all over the place. "Don't touch me!" She yelled.

The entire class turned to her, looking at her like she was a crazy woman.

Mr. Nelson didn't know how to react. "I'm sorry, I didn't mean to scare you."

Nita felt the urge to vomit coming fast. She got up, rushing past him, and running out of the classroom. She ran down the hall to the nearest restroom, rushing inside the first stall, throwing up immediately. Her insides felt like they were burning.

I can't do this.

She wiped her mouth, getting up and walking to the sink to clean herself up. She splashed water over her face, tying her hair up in a ponytail before heading back to class. She didn't want to go back, but she had too. She didn't want him to get suspicious. She made her way back to the classroom slowly, as Mr. Nelson was writing on the board. He got quiet as soon as she walked in. everyone staring at her.

"Feeling better Ms. Matua?" He asked.

"Yeah, I just had a bug, that's all."

"Freak." She heard coming from the back of the classroom. Her classmates laughed. Nita stood there, embarrassed.

"Hey! That's enough!" Mr. Nelson yelled at his students to quiet down. "Take a seat Amanita."

She walked back to her seat, not making eye contact with anyone. The afternoon couldn't come fast enough. She just wanted to get this day over with.

AT TWO-FORTY-FIVE, Nita sat in the library, waiting for the book club to begin. It was only her, and four other students that were in the club. Before the other students arrived, Ms. Stone came in.

"Amanita, it's so great to see you here! We've missed you being a part of the group." Ms. Stone said cheerfully.

"Thank you. It's great to be back."

"Don't forget, I still owe you that pizza." She said, winking at Nita with a smile.

The other four students showed up right after, taking their seats. They were continuing with *The Fire Beneath*. Nita had read the book already, so it didn't even matter that she missed most of the meetings.

"Today I wanted to discuss chapter thirteen when Orula starts to suspect that her husband is having an affair."

Everyone opened their books, following Ms. Stone's lead.

"Given everything she's going through, it's the last thing, someone, in her position would want to find out. That someone you love and trust is unimaginably betraying you." Mrs. Stone continued.

This made Nita think of Adrian. She could relate all too well to Orula right now.

"After finishing this chapter, how did it make you guys feel?" Ms. Stone asked.

She went around the group getting everyone's feedback.

"I felt bad for her. I couldn't believe that her husband would be sleeping around with someone else, especially after their child died." One of the girls said.

"I agree." Ms. Stone added.

"You'd be surprised." Nita interrupted. Everyone looked at her. "You never know people as well as you think you do. People you love will betray you, lie, keep things from you. Lead completely different lives and it'll hit you when you least expect it."

"You don't think her husband had his reasons? He was emotionally vulnerable. People have been known to do some pretty crazy things when they are suffering." Said Ms. Stone.

"That's no excuse." Said, Nita. She thought about how Ms. Stone would react if it turned out that Mr. Nelson was Chin, and if she would give him the same empathy as the man in the story.

"People deserve second chances." Said Ms. Stone.

We'll see about that. Nita thought.

Her and Nita locked eyes. Since Nita has read the book already, she didn't want to spoil it for the others.

"Well, maybe you're right. Hopefully, in the end, he'll redeem himself, and Orula will forgive him so they can live happily ever after." Nita was hoping Ms. Stone picked up on her sarcasm.

"Yes, let's hope so." Ms. Stone replied.

She looked over at the clock, and it read three-fifteen. Almost time for her to make her move.

"I gotta pee, I'll be right back." She told Ms. Stone.

"Sure." She replied.

Nita got up and made her way toward Mr. Nelson's classroom. She peeked inside, making sure the classroom was empty before she went in. She opened the door, quickly walking over to his desk, and opening the drawer on the left. It was full of pens, paper clips, and sticky note pads. She pushed it all aside, pulling the pill bag out of her pocket and placing it inside. She covered it up with all the pens and note pads and closed the drawer. Before leaving the classroom, she opened the door, peeking out in the hallway to make sure it was clear for her to walk out. She hurried out, closing the door behind her and walking back to the library.

For the remainder of the meeting, she didn't think about anything but what she had just done. For the sake of her sanity, she was hoping that Mr. Nelson turned out to be Chin, then all of this would be over. On the other hand, she was hoping he wasn't, because she didn't want to believe it. Either way, she was about to ruin a man's life, and his career. Tomorrow was going to be tough.

16
The Waiting Game

The weather was warm, like a humid evening in the middle of summer. Nita sat in the sand with her legs out straight, the cold water from the tide splashing against her feet. Adrian sat behind her, with his arms wrapped around her shoulders and his chin resting on her head. The beach was empty, just them and the soft breeze of the wind against the waves.

"It's so nice to have the beach to ourselves. No crowd, no volleyballs hitting me in the head." Said Nita, giggling.

"Yes, it is nice," Adrian replied.

Nita caressed his hands as he held her in his arms. "I love you, Adrian."

"I love you too, Nita."

"I wish we could just stay here forever, just the two of us." She said, wiggling her toes in the wet sand.

"We can. I can fish for food, and we can build a little hut underneath the dock, in the shade." He laughed, his bright white smile reflecting off the sun.

"You're so silly." Nita laughed along with him. Her happiness quickly turned into sadness. "What happens after all this? When you leave for college? What happens to us?"

"Nothing happens to us. I may be far away, but I'll never be gone." Adrian moved her hair away from the side of her face, gently kissing her on the cheek. "I'll never leave you, don't worry."

"Promise?"

"I promise."

Nita woke up. A few seconds later, her alarm clock went off. For the first time in months, she had a normal dream. A dream about Adrian, where they were happy. In another time where this nightmare of reality didn't exist. This was also the first time in months, where she wanted to go back to sleep, and maybe never wake up. She slammed her hand over her alarm, knocking it on the floor. Her eyes were still puffy from all the crying from the night before. After what she did to Mr. Nelson, her heart couldn't take it. She knew it was what she had to do, but unless he turned out to be Chin, she didn't know how she would ever live with herself. Her cell phone started to ring, she grabbed it from her night-stand. It was Benjamin. Her stomach started to hurt.

"Hey."

"Turn on the news! Channel four!"

Without saying another word, Nita sat up, grabbed her remote, and turned to the channel. It was breaking news coverage at Orchard Valley High School. There were police cars and camera crews every-where.

Breaking News here at Orchard Valley High, where thirty-two-year-old Edward Nelson, a Chemistry teacher has been arrested for drug pos-session. This comes as a shock to the entire faculty at this Wicomico high school. More details soon...

Nita watched as Mr. Nelson was hauled off in handcuffs. His head down in shame, as teachers and other school staff members, watched in shock.

"So... now what?" Nita asked.

"Well, we wait. They're probably searching his house already. If he really is Chin, it will come out. It has too."

"I hope you're right."

There was a knock on her bedroom door. She knew what her par-ents wanted, they had most likely heard the news already. "I'll call you right back." She quickly hung up on Benjamin before telling them they could come in.

"Amanita, I see you've caught the news already." Her father said, looking at the TV.

"Yeah, I know. I can't believe it."

"I'm so sorry honey. I know he was one of your favorites." Her mother walked over to her bedside.

"I would've never thought. He seemed like a decent guy." Robert added.

"I'm just as shocked as you," Latisha said to Robert. She hugged Nita. "Sweetie, you don't have to go to school today. It's probably a circus. I'd rather you stay home and not be involved in all of that."

"Yeah, I think I'll stay home." Nita was glad her mother said it first because if there was one place she didn't want to be that day, it was school.

"The more time passes, the more I start to feel like we need to move." Her father shook his head, still looking at the TV.

"If it were that easy, we would've been out of here months ago. You know that." Latisha gave her husband an indignant look. "If you need us, we'll be downstairs." She told Nita, then walked toward the door with Robert.

"Let me know if you want to go by the hospital, today sweetheart," Robert added.

"Okay, dad." She smiled.

As soon as her parents left her room, she immediately called Benjamin back.

"I'm guessing your parents heard?"

"Yeah."

"You're not going to school, today are you?"

"No, my mom said I could stay home. I couldn't stand to be there today anyway." Nita laid back down, staring up at the ceiling. "What if the cops don't find anything that links Mr. Nelson to all this?"

"I don't know. Then that means Chin is still out there I guess... Let's just wait and see how this plays out. That's all we can do."

Nita's eyes started to fill with tears. "I don't know how much more of any of this I can take. It's driving me crazy and I just feel like I'm burying myself deeper and deeper into all of it."

Benjamin sighed heavily into the phone. "Everything will be alright."

"Promise?" She said.

"Promise."

NITA SLEPT FOR MOST of the day. She went downstairs to get lunch and took a shower afterward, but that was the only time she left her room. She watched Maury reruns, played mobile games on her phone, and refreshed news pages, waiting to see if there were any updates about Mr. Nelson. But there was nothing. The anticipation was killing her. Mostly because there would be no guarantee that this plan would play out immediately. It could be days, or weeks before the cops found anything if they found anything. Her depression started to take over, and she decided to get some sleep, to take a break from her thoughts.

Her phone rang. It was five o'clock in the evening. It was Benjamin. She rolled over on her side to answer it.

"Hey, Ben."

"Nita, we did it."

She sprung up from the covers. She wasn't sure if she had heard him correctly. "What?"

"We did it! The news, turn it on! They got him!"

Nita fumbled around the bed for her remote and her hands trembled as she turned on her TV, flipping to channel four. Mr. Nelson's mugshot was in the upper right corner as the reporter spoke.

Thirty-two-year-old Edward Nelson, a teacher at Orchard Valley High School who was arrested this morning with drug possession when illegal pills were found in his classroom, has just been charged with drug possession with intent to sell. This comes after authorities found more drugs in his home, along with thousands of dollars and illegal weapons. He is being held on a 25,000 bail. We will keep you updated on this story.

Nita was speechless. She couldn't believe it.

"It's all over now. Wow, it really was him, all this time." Said, Benjamin.

Nita just sat there, silent, taking it all in. Mr. Nelson, a man whom she thought so highly of, was a man who was responsible for the murder of three people, maybe more than that. Behind those kind eyes, he was a monster. She then remembered about Ms. Stone. "Oh no, Ms. Stone must be crushed. Poor woman."

"Yeah, I know. I feel so bad for her. She must be taking this pretty hard."

"She's probably going to quit now, this must be so humiliating for her." Nita felt bad for her teacher, but at the same time, she knew Ms. Stone was better off without him.

"You think she knew?" Ben asked.

"No way! I seriously doubt she had a clue."

"So, how do you feel?"

Nita felt a million things at once. Overwhelmed, shocked, relieved, heavyhearted, but only one feeling mattered at that moment. "I feel, satisfied."

17
The Fire Beneath

Nita sat at the breakfast table with her parents the following morning. Her father had the television from the living room up at a high volume while he watched the news. The news stations had been doing non-stop coverage on Mr. Nelson. This had been the biggest news story since Adrian's murder. Nita sat at the table, eating her breakfast, while her mother sat across from her, drinking her coffee and reading about the same news coverage on her phone.

"First a drug dealer, now they're saying he killed some people. Wow, man." Robert yelled from the living room.

"Well, if he's a drug dealer, then are you surprised that he's killed, people?" Her mother said to him. She then looked at Nita. "Wasn't he dating someone at the school? That's what one of the news stories said."

Nita stopped chewing on her sausage and looked up at her mother. "Yeah. My English teacher. Carmen Stone."

"That poor woman. She must be devastated. I know the cops have been on her like white on rice." Latisha said, her facial expression empathetic. She knew all too well from the family's experience after Adrian's murder.

The news went to commercial, and Robert walked into the kitchen. "Poor woman? There is no way you date a man like that and not know what he's up too." He said, grabbing a cup from the cabinet to make coffee.

"You don't know that," Latisha replied.

"She's right dad, you don't know that." Nita was already tired of their conversation. "Can you guys not talk about it anymore? Not right now anyway."

"I'm sorry honey. We didn't mean to make you upset." Her mother grabbed her hand from across.

"It's fine, I've just heard enough about it for a day. I'm already going to have to deal with it when I go back to school on Monday."

It wasn't just that. Nita was planning on going to the police and telling them everything. About finding the drugs in Adrian's room, Max, the apartment, the blonde woman. This also meant coming clean to her parents. After her short feeling of relief, the night before, she knew that this wasn't over yet. The cops would most likely link Mr. Nelson to the blonde woman's murder, but not necessarily Adrian, or even Max. Max's death was still ruled a suicide, and there was no evidence pointing to any involvement with drugs in Adrian's death. The only way to truly get justice for them was to reveal herself. She wasn't sure if this meant she would be charged with anything, but she was willing to pay the price, whatever it was.

"I'm going to go upstairs and get dressed. I want to see Benjamin today." Nita got up from her chair.

"Sure. Just let us know when you're ready." Her father said.

Nita tossed her plate into the sink and hurried up to her room to call Benjamin. She wanted to tell him what she was planning to do before she went to see him. She knew he'd be mad and wanted to avoid him making a scene. She went inside and sat on her bed, grabbing her phone from the charger.

"Good morning beautiful!" He answered cheerfully.

"Hey."

He picked up on her mood immediately. "You don't sound so happy. What's wrong?"

"I'm going to do it. Today."

"Do what?"

"I'm going to see Detective Jackson. I'm telling her everything."

"What!? No!"

"Ben, I have too. It's the only way to end things for good. I've got to do it for Max, and Adrian, and myself. For you too. You're in the hospital because of him, remember?"

"So, what? You're going to go in there and tell them that you planted drugs on him? Don't be stupid Nita."

"Well, maybe not that. I don't know yet. But they must at least know we found drugs in Adrian's room. Also, Max told me about the address because I was curious. That's all they need to know."

"You've been questioned by the cops before, you should know that's not all they are going to want to know. You could go to jail. *WE* could!"

"No, you won't. I won't even mention that you were involved."

"Now you're crazy if you think I'm going to let you take the blame for this all this by yourself."

Nita smiled. This is why she loved Benjamin so much. "Ben, I'm scared." Even though she accepted that this is what she needed to do, her bravery didn't erase her fear of the consequences that may come.

"Don't be scared. We're the victims in this. We didn't do anything wrong. Besides planting the drugs, but the cops don't have to know that. Plus, Mr. Nelson is guilty anyway, so what difference would it make?"

Nita felt a sense of assurance from what he was saying. "You're right."

There was a short pause between them. "If you're going to do this, then wait for me. Even if I must sneak out of here, we're going together."

"I appreciate your effort Ben, but I can call the detective and have her come up to the hospital. We're coming up there in a little bit by the way."

"Wait, before we do this, there is one more thing you have to do."

"What?"

"You have to go back to the school and put that journal back in Max's locker."

Nita had forgotten about the journal. The last thing she needed was evidence laying around her house. She looked at the time on her phone. It was nine-twelve. The school would be open for Saturday detention, so she had an open opportunity to put the journal back without getting caught.

"I'll go now. I'll text you when we're on our way to the hospital."

"Alright."

"Talk to you soon. Thanks for being there for me Ben."

"Love you Amanita."

"Love you too."

They hung up, and Nita quickly threw on a pair of shorts and a top, grabbing her sneakers and then grabbing the journal from under her bed. She went downstairs and told her parents that she wanted to go for a quick walk before heading to the hospital.

"I don't think that's a good idea. I still don't feel too comfortable with you being out by yourself." Her father protested.

"Dad, it's therapeutic. Besides, I won't go too far. Twenty minutes, that's all I need." She tried to get as pathetic as possible, so he would let her go. "With everything going on with my teacher, I just want to clear my head." She said, with her head down, trying to look as sorrowful as she could.

"Twenty minutes." Her father said, nodding in approval. He couldn't resist Nita's puppy dog eyes whenever she wanted something.

"Love you guys. Be right back." She hurried out the door with the journal tucked under her hoodie. Luckily it was flimsy and went unnoticeable.

She arrived at the school, only a few cars were in the parking lot. She went around to the back, so she could go in through the back doors. Once inside, she made her way to the second floor, to Max's locker. The lock was still open, so she stuffed the journal inside and got out of there as quickly as she could. walking down the hall, she noticed one classroom with the light on. It was Ms. Stone's classroom. Nita knew she needed to head home, but she couldn't help but stop by to see if her teacher as okay. She walked up toward the door, and Ms. Stone had a big brown box on her desk. She was packing her things.

"Ms. Stone?" Nita said softly. She still managed to startle her while her back was turned.

"Amanita? What are you doing here?" Ms. Stone looked confused to see her, pausing in the middle of her packing, adjusting her glasses.

"Oh, nothing. I was just... stopping by to get some things from my locker. I saw your light on, and just wanted to see if you were alright."

Ms. Stone smiled slightly. "I'm holding up. Thanks for asking."

The tension started to feel awkward. "I'm sorry about Mr. Nelson," Nita said.

"It's alright. After spending my night being questioned by detectives, and my phone ringing like crazy from friends and staff wanting to talk to me, I think I'm holding up pretty well." She went back to packing.

Nita watched, realizing what this meant. Ms. Stone was quitting. Nita hated to see her go, she enjoyed Ms. Stone, as an educator, and a fellow book lover.

"Ms. Stone, I'm going to miss you. I wish you didn't have to go."

Ms. Stone paused again. "I'll miss you too Amanita. It's a very unfortunate situation for me and my students. But it's not a good idea for me to be here anymore, I'm sure you understand, hopefully, everyone else will too." She walked over to her. "You know, I never got to take you out for that pizza I promised."

"Oh, that's alright."

"No, I must. I owe you. Besides, I'm leaving town tomorrow morning, and this is the last time you'll see me."

Now Nita felt bad. Since this would be the last time she saw her, she figured it wouldn't hurt. "Well, Roberto's isn't that far. I gotta be home soon, but I can take it to go." Nita smiled.

"Good. Just let me grab my purse. We can discuss *The Fire Beneath* on the way." She winked at Nita. Grabbing her purse and turning off the light.

Roberto's was about an eight-minute drive from the school. Breaking the awkward silence during the drive, Ms. Stone mentioned *The Fire Beneath*.

"You know, you were right about what you said, Nita."

"About?"

"During book club, you said that we don't always know people as well as we think we do. You were right."

Nita didn't know what to say. "So, I assume that means you finished the book?"

"Yes, I did. Didn't see that ending coming."

"You finished the book before everyone else, you broke the rules of book club!" Nita said, laughing.

"Hey! You read it already! You're one to talk!" Ms. Stone laughed too.

"It's my favorite book. I've read it a bunch of times." Nita admitted.

As Ms. Stone drove, Nita looked around her car. It was nice and clean. She had cute little bobbleheads on the dashboard. One of the bobbleheads was a little man, with big glasses and a lab coat giving thumbs up. Below his feet, there were big bold letters that read, *IRVING SCIENCE ACADEMY CHEMISTRY HONORS.*

"Chemistry? I didn't know you went to school for science." Nita asked, extremely curious.

"There is a lot you don't know about me, Amanita." Ms. Stone said with a dull tone, staring at the road.

Nita didn't understand. "Huh?"

"You are an intelligent, beautiful girl, Amanita. It's a shame I have to kill you."

Nita didn't even have time to react before Ms. Stone struck her in the side of the neck with a sharp object. Nita could hear her heart beating, slowly through her chest. Her vision went blurry. She reached for the object, still stuck in the side of her neck. It was a syringe. Nita started breathing heavily, in shock looking at Ms. Stone who was still staring at the road, driving. She didn't seem at all phased by what she had just done. Nita tried to reach for the door, but whatever she had been injected with had already been working its way into her system. It was too late.

18
It Was Her

Nita woke up to an excruciating headache. She felt weak, her vision still a bit blurry as she opened her eyes. For a quick second, she had forgotten about what had happened. But that didn't last long. Within seconds the memory came back to her. She suddenly became overwhelmed with shock as she tried to scream, realizing that her mouth was taped shut. She wiggled around frantically, her hands tied together with the same duct tape that was used around her mouth. Her legs were the same. She looked around to see where she was. It was dark and cold. There was nothing but pipes, covered in mold. The smell was horrific. It was a basement. She still attempted to scream through the duct tape but knew her muffled cries would be no help. She was alone, and afraid, and helpless in an unknown place. The only thing worse than death for her was living out her days in seclusion, never seeing anyone she loved or cared about ever again.

A few moments later, she heard footsteps. She couldn't see from the angle she was sitting, but she could tell by the sound that they were coming down a set of stairs.

"Oh good, you're awake. It's about time. I was getting impatient and ready to just kill you while you were out, but that wouldn't have been fun." Ms. Stone said walking over to Nita.

The neat bun she usually wore was undone, and her blonde hair draped over shoulders. She had a gun in her right hand, with a pocket knife sticking out of her left pants pocket. She was also no longer wearing her glasses. Nita looked at her, not recognizing this woman anymore. This woman standing in front of her was a stranger. A sweet, innocent woman who loved to read, ate her cupcakes with a fork and never said so much as a mild swear word. This woman had just kidnapped a minor and was about to kill her. Ms. Stone walked up to Nita, bending down in front of her. Nita began to scream again, turning her face away. Ms. Stone grabbed the duct tape and snatched it off her mouth. Nita screamed out in pain.

"Oh, stop being dramatic." Ms. Stone rolled her eyes and walked over to another side of the basement to grab a chair. She dragged it over, sitting it in front of Nita, taking a seat. She wanted to be face-to-face.

"Help! Help me, somebody! Please!"

"No one can hear you. That should be obvious. I don't even know why I bothered to tape your mouth shut. Dramatic effect I guess?" Ms. Stone laughed with an evil smile on her face.

"Please don't kill me," Nita begged, her face wet from tears.

"I won't, not yet anyway. I still need a few things sorted out before I get out of town. So, you have a good thirty more minutes or so if you're lucky. Kidnapping you was honestly not a part of my plan. Well, not today. If you would've just let me take you out for Pizza when I asked the first time I could've taken care of you then. But, I guess today was your lucky day."

Nita began crying hysterically. "Please, please!" she pleaded.

Ms. Stone got up, leaning down toward Nita. She grabbed her jaw roughly, her mildly sharp manicured nails digging into her skin.

"Stop crying Amanita. You bought this on yourself. You really thought you could go snooping around with no consequences?"

"My parents... they'll be looking for me!" Nita uttered through Ms. Stone's tight grip.

"They won't find you here. The police can search all night and day and they still wouldn't find this place. It's an abandoned property my brother bought six years ago. We use it to... do business."

Ms. Stone sat back down, with a menacing look across her face as she put the pistol away inside her pants. Nita knew exactly what she meant by that. She was about to become another victim. "Oh, and you met my brother by the way. He was working with Eva, you remember her."

Nita looked at her in shock. "You're Chin."

"I'm Chin, we're all Chin. The name is from me, but we all carry it. I thought of it when I started selling rippers after college. I eventually moved on to harder drugs, but those pills have always been a good money maker. Every one of my dealers goes by the name Chin. That way, Chin can be everywhere, all the time."

Nita then remembered about Mr. Nelson and wondered where he fit into all of this. "Mr. Nelson."

Ms. Stone's wicked facial expression suddenly became somber at the mention of his name.

"Oh Edward, poor bastard. I really did love him you know." Her expression softened. "We met three years ago when we were both teaching science at a middle school in Orange County. Things used to be amazing with us, but he was a mess. He must've found out about rippers going around and wanted to use them as a boost while he worked on a science project. It was going to be award-worthy research too. Too bad he was stupid enough to leave them on school property."

Ms. Stone didn't know about the setup. But this meant that Mr. Nelson was buying drugs after all. So, Nita planting the drugs was good timing. She was crushed, realizing that he was innocent after all. Him buying the drugs must've been how they got his confession.

"That idiot confessed to everything. He told the cops that the drugs found, weren't his, but the guilt from buying them was too much for him to handle, so he admitted to that. They broke him so easily after that."

Nita could see the heartbreak in her eyes.

"I never told him about any of this." Mrs. Stone continued. "He didn't even know he was buying from my brother. When we went on vacation a year ago, I got my men to plant my stuff in his house, just in case things went south. I knew he was weak, and business was business."

Nita couldn't believe what she was hearing. The betrayal was revolting. But Mr. Nelson was sitting in jail, and there was nothing she could do about it. Hearing all this information, there was only one detail Nita really cared about. Adrian.

"Why did you kill him?" Nita asked. "Adrian. Why did you kill Adrian.?"

Ms. Stone's eyes drifted towards the floor.

"Adrian. He started working for me in his junior year. I found out he was cheating on his exams to keep his grades up for basketball. I was going to have him expelled, ruining any chance he had at a college basketball career but decided to use this opportunity to help my business. At first, he loved the money. Four hundred a week to pick up my product and deliver it to all my locations. But eventually, he got tired of it. He wanted out, but I told him he worked for me until I said otherwise."

"You didn't have to kill him!" Nita shot back.

"He threatened to expose me, stealing some of my pills. I found out and had to take him out myself." Mrs. Stone had the pocket knife in her hand, twirling the blade around with her fingertip. "Watching him die felt so damn good. That's what happens when you get in my way when you don't play your part and fall out of line. I end you!"

She tossed the knife on the floor, pulling out the pistol and aiming it dead at Nita's forehead. Nita realized she was staring death in the face. A chill crept up her spine, and her heart was beating fast. It was like that night at the apartment all over again. But this time, there were no second chances. She thought about her family, about Benjamin and how she would never see them again. It was a pain worse than death itself.

"I trusted you," Nita mumbled with trembling lips.

"Yeah, well, maybe you shouldn't have."

Right as Ms. Stone clenched the trigger, there was a sudden creaking sound coming from upstairs. It sounded like footsteps. Someone was there. Ms. Stone looked up at the ceiling, her face stunned. She had no idea who it was. Only her brother and a few drug associates knew about the house, and her brother knew that she had taken Nita there to kill her, but she knew he would've warned her ahead of time if he were coming.

"Shut up, I'll be right back." Ms. Stone grabbed the duct tape that was sitting nearby and put a fresh piece of tape over Nita's mouth.

She went upstairs quietly, her gun drawn, to check out the noise. As soon as Nita heard the door close, she immediately started wiggling her arms and legs, to loosen up the duct tape. It wouldn't budge, and she became frustrated. She felt hopeless and terrified, knowing that it would all be over the minute Ms. Stone returned. Nita gave up, her head down, feeling defeated. Then she noticed the knife on the floor that Ms. Stone had tossed. It wasn't too far from her reach if she tried hard enough. She used her feet and scooted herself up, getting close enough to throw herself over it, grabbing it with her fingers which weren't completely covered in the tape. She grabbed the blade, attempting to cut away at the tape. All she needed was to get the knife halfway through, and she could break away from the rest. She rapidly sliced away at the tape, repeatedly poking herself in the process. It was painful, but she wouldn't stop until she was free. When she felt that she had sliced a good amount of tape, she used the little strength she had left to break through the rest. She could hear it rip instantly, getting a jolt of relief when she realized it had worked. She didn't even bother pulling the rest of the tape from her hands and wrists before cutting the tape from her legs and feet. She was free, but then the feeling of relief turned to fear as she realized that she didn't have much time. She could've made a run for the stairs and out of the basement, but it was too risky. She looked around to see where she could hide. She saw a small space behind what looked like a furnace and ran over, slouching down behind it.

Upstairs, Ms. Stone had made her way quietly from behind the basement door, and into the next room, which was an empty wide-open area. She saw a young man, who looked to be in his early twenties standing a few feet away, with his cell phone in his hand. He was so focused on his phone, he didn't even see Ms. Stone approaching him. He didn't seem like an immediate threat, so she put her gun away in the back of her pants.

"Are you lost?" She said, standing a few feet away from him. He jumped, not expecting to see anyone else around.

"Oh! I didn't realize someone else was here." The young man looked surprised to see her. "Are you looking for the gold water dragon too?" He asked excitedly.

Ms. Stone was confused. "What?"

"Creature Catch. You know, the game? My app notified me that there was a gold water dragon in here."

Ms. Stone didn't respond, just stood there giving him an irritated look. His excitement turned to worry as he realized that this woman wasn't there catching creatures and that he had possibly walked in on something that he shouldn't have.

"Umm... I guess my app was wrong. I'm just gonna go." He started to back away.

Ms. Stone knew what she had to do. "I'm sorry sweetheart."

She pulled out her gun and shot him twice in the chest. He fell to the floor. The shots were fatal. Ms. Stone didn't want to kill him, but he was in the wrong place at the wrong time, and she couldn't risk a witness. She walked back to the basement, with her pistol still in hand. She walked over to the spot where Nita was and saw that she had gotten free. She panicked for a second but realized that Nita didn't have the time to escape the basement, so she knew she was still there. She laughed.

"You can't get away from me Amanita. There is nowhere for you to go."

Nita just hid quietly, panicking. She knew she needed a plan, and fast. Ms. Stone walked around slowly, her gun out and ready to fire at the sight of Nita. She walked toward the furnace, Nita standing there, holding the knife close to her chest. The furnace wasn't lit, Ms.

Stone opened it, thinking that Nita had hidden inside. Nita took this as an opportunity to fight back, and charged at her, wielding the knife and catching Ms. Stone off guard, stabbing her in the back. Ms. Stone screamed out in pain, dropping her gun, and stumbling backward. Nita ran toward the stairs, but the stab wound she gave Ms. Stone wasn't enough to keep her down. She pulled the knife from her back, and ran after Nita, grabbing her leg and dragging her back down before she could get halfway up. Nita kicked her, but Ms. Stone stabbed her in the ankle, causing Nita to fall. Ms. Stone climbed over her, angry, her eyes filled with rage. She stabbed Nita in the stomach, her, screaming out in agonizing pain. Ms. Stone wrapped her bloody hands around Nita's neck squeezing with every bit of energy she had.

"I was there. I was there when you found him. Dead, in a pool of his own blood." The veins from Ms. Stone's head and hands were visible, her blue eyes were big and sinister. She had gone full-blown psychotic as she strangled Nita. "I saw you standing there, like a scared little puppy hanging over his cold lifeless body. I was going to kill you too, but I couldn't do it. I felt sorry for you, so I just left. But now, I'm wishing I had just done it."

Tears made their way to the surface as Nita felt herself losing strength. She clawed at Ms. Stone's hands but knew it was no use. Her will to live wasn't strong enough anymore. Ms. Stone started smiling in satisfaction as she watched Nita accept her death.

"Freeze!" A loud female voice yelled from the top of the steps.

It was Detective Jackson. "Make another move and I'll shoot you, Carmen, I mean it!" Detective Jackson aimed her gun directly at Ms. Stone. "Get the paramedics here, now!"

She made a head gesture and two uniformed officers came down and pulled Ms. Stone off Nita. They slapped the cuffs on her wrists, as Detective Jackson came to Nita's aid.

"Carmen Stone, you have the right to remain silent. Anything you say can be used against you. You have the right to an attorney. If you cannot afford one, one will be appointed to you by the court..."

The uniformed officers dragged Ms. Stone up the stairs as she was read her rights.

Detective Jackson sat there, with Nita coughing and gagging as she recovered. "We were right on time."

19

Life Again

At the hospital, Nita sat as the nurse finished up the stitches in her ankle wound after finishing up with the knife wound. Fortunately, the stab to her stomach missed major organs and wasn't life-threatening. When Nita hadn't returned home after half an hour, her parents got worried and called Benjamin. That's when he told them about the journal. They drove up to the school and when Nita was nowhere to be found they immediately called the police. Detective Jackson told them that Nita had to be missing for forty-eight hours before they could declare her missing, but Benjamin told them nearly everything. About the drugs in Adrian's room, Max, the blonde woman, and their visit to Baker's rd. The only thing he left out was their plan to plant the drugs. He and Nita had agreed that they would only reveal that if it was necessary. When he told detective Jackson about Nita returning the journal, she agreed that it was no coincidence that Nita was missing, and dispatched officers to check in and around the school. One of the students that were there for detention told the cops they saw Nita leaving with Ms. Stone. It wasn't long before they investigated Ms. Stone's background and found out about her brother, the short man. The police located him, bringing him in for questioning. He had a previous record, and they used prior drug charges to threaten him into telling them everything to avoid jail time. He told Detective Jackson about the house. She and a few of her officers were getting close to the house when they heard the gunshots from Ms. Stone killing the young man, leading them right to her.

Nita's parents were devastated to hear about what their daughter had just gone through and to know that it was a teacher, someone she knew and trusted. Through all of that, they were thankful and happy that she was found safe.

"It was pretty deep, but you should be fine." The nurse told Nita.

"We're so glad you're safe. I don't know what we would've done if we had lost you." Latisha grabbed her daughter and hugged her tightly.

"I would've killed her myself." Benjamin chimed in.

"Well, that woman is going to be rotting in jail, where she belongs." Robert stood next to his wife, comforting his daughter.

"What about Mr. Nelson?" Nita asked.

"The police said that Ms. Stone may have put the drugs in his classroom, to frame him. He did confess to buying drugs, so he'll still be investigated. Hopefully, things work out for him in the end." Said Robert.

Her mother placed her hand on Nita's shoulder. "They're also re-opening Adrian and Max's cases. Sweetie, you know this means you'll have to testify."

"I'll be right there with you," Benjamin assured her. "We're in this together."

Nita knew this wasn't over, and there was still more to do, to make sure Ms. Stone never saw the light of day again. But with the support of her family and her best friend, she knew everything would be okay.

THE BLUE IRISES AND Hydrangea's that covered the walls were particularly calming this day. Nita sat in the waiting room of the Braxton-Grove Wellness Center waiting for her appointment. Nita told her parents that she wanted to start going back to therapy again, once a week. She knew getting her life back would involve taking some personal responsibility for her own mental health. Her mother sat next to her, reading a magazine. She turned to Nita.

"I'm glad you're doing this. I'm proud of you." She told her daughter.

The door from the back opened and Dr. Braxton called for Nita. She got up, walking to the back, and taking a deep breath. She took her usual seat on the nude-colored love chair as Dr. Braxton sat across from her in the metal chair, note pad and pen in hand.

"It's nice to see you Amanita. I hear you have a court case coming up. You've been through a lot these past few weeks."

"Yes, I'm nervous but ready."

"How have your dreams been?" Dr. Braxton asked.

"Some good, some bad. Some I don't even remember when I wake up."

"That's okay. Tell me more about them..."

Nita described her dreams vividly to Dr. Braxton, they discussed her feelings about the upcoming case against her teacher and the aftermath of her kidnapping. It would take time, but she would have her peace and her life back again.

Here's a special treat! Check out the first chapter from River's Moonlight!

What started out as a casual date between two teenagers, ends in terror for seventeen-year-old River Lewis. A near death experience leads to strange and unimaginable behaviors, and changes in her physical appearance that transform her life forever. With the help of a new friend, a young man named Jax, River must learn to adapt to her new life, a double life. But with bodies piling up on the streets of Chicago and her aunt being in charge of investigating these mysterious murders, learning to tame the beast inside won't be River's only problem. Part one of the 'Moonlight Series'.

Chapter 1

"**H**e's beautiful! I love him!" River ran her fingers through the chocolate lab's smooth brown fur. He barked and jumped up and down in excitement as he enjoyed the embrace of his new owners. River loved dogs, and seeing this adorable surprise sitting on the sofa when she arrived home from school was the highlight of her day.

"He was just walking along the freeway. No collar, nothing." Her aunt Tasha stood there scratching her head, with one hand on her hip as she watched River interact with the pup. "I was going to call animal control, but I figured he could use a nice home."

"Well, I'm glad you didn't call them. Poor thing would've been put down. You did something nice for once. I'm proud of you." River said sarcastically. Tasha picked up on River's sarcasm immediately and shot a nasty look at her niece. River just smiled at her and continued giving her attention to the dog. Tasha wanted to respond to River's smart remark but decided to let it slide.

She and River didn't have the best relationship. When River was nine years old, she survived a car accident, but her parents weren't so lucky. Since then, she had been raised by her aunt Tasha. Growing up without her mother and father caused River to shut out anyone who tried to get close to her. Her aunt tried to fill the emotional void of River's loss of a mother figure, but it just caused River to loathe her more. It also didn't help that Tasha was a cop, which made her extremely assertive and oftentimes aggressive. Her tough personality clashing with River's teenage angst caused bad vibes between them. Her aunt being a cop also made it hard for River to socialize. Not too many people on the south side of Chicago wanted to be friends with a girl who lived with a cop.

"Alright now." Tasha huffed. "He better not mess up my house. I just got this carpet steam cleaned. You train him to do his business outside or off to the pound he goes." Tasha had a hard time letting things go, she was passive-aggressive and held grudges which contributed to her complicated relationship with River.

"Well, you brought him home. If he messes up the carpet, it's your fault." River instantly became annoyed. Her aunt brought the dog home because she wanted to but was willing to get rid of him just to spite her.

"I said what I said." Tasha shot back.

"Come on boy, let's get you some fresh air." River took the dog out to the backyard and let him run around while she tossed a stick across the yard for him to fetch. The clouds were forming close together, and the wind began to pick up. He brought the stick back and dropped it at her feet. He moaned and rubbed his head against her leg. She caressed his face. "What's wrong buddy? Miss your family?"

Trying to comfort the dog made her think about her parents. What her life would be like if they were still alive. She had these thoughts often, but they just led to depressive episodes that made her feel worse. It's not that she wasn't grateful for her aunt taking her in, she really did care for her and appreciated everything she had done for her. But despite her aunt's attempts to be a parental figure, she couldn't replace her mom. "I guess we've got something in common then." Her soft touch got the dog excited again, jumping in her lap and licking her face. For once, it would feel nice having someone in the house that she could relate to, that could love her unconditionally. "I think I'll name you Coco." She allowed the dog to lick her face, while he playfully signaled for her to continue throwing the stick.

River's phone rang, and she grabbed it from her left pocket to see who it was. It was Andrew. A friend from school who she was going out with that night. She didn't typically like to date, but Andrew was cute and had been begging her to go see a movie with him since the school year started. She finally gave in and accepted. She decided not to answer the call, just to keep him guessing. River liked being a tease. It was entertaining for her to watch simple-minded teenage boys like Andrew fall for her puerile ways. She knew he'd be blowing up her messages any second now. She was right. Not even thirty seconds after the phone stopped ringing, she got a text notification.

Drew: *We still on for tonight? Can't wait to see you.*

River smiled at the message and decided to wait a few minutes before replying. She grabbed Coco by the collar and pulled him toward the back door. "Come on buddy, I've got a date tonight. Time to go inside."

Back inside, she noticed Tasha putting on her jacket, preparing to leave. "Going back to work already?" River asked.

"Yeah, got a call from Juarez. Body found behind the bodega on 13th street. It's bad. I've gotta go."

"Another shooting? Can't they handle it without you? Shootings aren't anything uncommon here."

Tasha gave River a tense look. "I didn't say it was a shooting. You know not to ask me questions about murder cases. I can't discuss this stuff with you, you know that."

River rolled her eyes. "Right, how could I forget."

"Look, I think you should stay in tonight." Tasha urged. River noticed that her aunt looked concerned.

"Stay in? Why? Murders happen every other day in this city. What's the big deal?"

"Just stay in tonight okay? Why do you have to be so damn hard-headed? Can't you just listen to me for once!" Tasha shouted. A vein emerged on the left side of her forehead. That only happened when she was pissed off or stressed out. Either way, something about work was bugging her. More than usual. River knew this wasn't a normal gang-related shooting.

"Fine. Whatever." River agreed.

"I'll be back." Tasha didn't say anything else before immediately walking out the door. River went upstairs to her room, with Coco following behind. She sat on her bed and pulled out her phone to text Andrew back.

River: *Yeah of course. Picking me up at 7, right?*

Not even twenty seconds later he replied.

Drew: *Yes! See you then!*

"Man, he sure doesn't waste any time." River said to herself, amused by Andrew's swiftness. She knew he really liked her. Most guys were attracted to her. Her light bronze skin complimented by her dark brown eyes, which she got from her Filipino mother. Her big, thick, jet-black coils came from her father's side. Whenever she wore her hair straight, River was a spitting image of her mother. Tasha and River's mother never got along, which contributed to River's strained relationship with Tasha. She knew every time her aunt looked at her, she saw her mother. A woman she only tolerated out of love for her brother, River's father.

River threw her phone on her nightstand and decided to take a short nap before her date with Andrew. Despite her aunt's wishes, she decided to go out anyway. She needed to get out of the house, even if she had to cut her date short to be back before her aunt got home. She got undressed, climbed under the covers with Coco joining her at the foot of the bed, and went to sleep.

River was awakened by Coco licking her face. She reached over to her bedside dresser to grab her phone and check the time. She realized it only had thirty-five percent battery life left, grunting at her phone and tossing it back on the dresser. It was six-thirty-eight in the evening, and she knew Andrew would be there soon. She kissed Coco on the nose and gently moved him out of the way, so she could get up. On her way to the bathroom to freshen up, she got a look at herself in the long wall mirror across from her bed. Her hair was frizzy from her nap, and she could see bags forming under her eyes. She knew she didn't have enough time to shower, but decided to take one anyway. Even if Andrew had to sit in his car and wait, River didn't care. She was doing him a favor by even agreeing to go out with him in the first place. He was cute, but she found him rather annoying at times. An extra ten minutes of waiting wouldn't hurt him.

After her shower, she braided her freshly washed hair back in four large French braids. She searched her closet for something to wear. River had a personality as tough as rocks and a rugged street style to match. She grabbed her dark blue skin-tight denim jeans with the thighs ripped slightly. Just enough to expose just a little of her caramel skin. She grabbed a blue and white striped tank top that exposed her belly button and threw her brown leather jacket over it. She heard the doorbell ring from downstairs. She knew it was Andrew. She glanced at the clock on her wall. It read six-fifty-three. She quickly grabbed her cell phone from the dresser and her black converse from the floor by her bedroom door before heading downstairs.

Andrew rang the doorbell two more times before River got to the door. She opened it, and there he stood. Tall, lean, and gorgeous with a huge smile on his face.

"Hey." He greeted with his deep, sultry voice.

"Hey good looking." She replied, smiling at him. Coco came running behind her, barking at Andrew. "Hey now, cut it out. He's cool." She rubbed Coco's face to calm him down.

Andrew looked at the dog, a bit intimidated. "You have a dog? That's cool, I guess." He said, expressing a lack of interest in her aggressive pet.

"Yeah, most people do." River teased. She guided Coco away and quickly closed the door behind her. She walked to the passenger's side of Andrew's car and opened it, jumping inside.

"I could've gotten that for you, ya know."

"Too slow bro!" River laughed. Once inside the driver's seat, Andrew placed his hand on River's thigh. He leaned over, signaling a kiss from her. "Whoa! I just got in the car. You haven't even gotten me anything to eat yet."

"Aww come on. I can't get a kiss?" He asked anxiously.

"A kiss?! Buy me some tacos first. Then we'll see what you get by the end of the night." River gazed him up and down with her mesmerizing brown eyes. Andrew couldn't resist the temptation.

"I like the sound of that." He sighed heavily. "Alright. Food it is." He started the car and drove away.

They decided to see a movie first, a horror film that had just been released that night. During the film, Andrew kept trying to get intimate with River, putting his arm around her shoulders, which she allowed. When he tried to lean in for a kiss, she brushed him off again. This agitated him, he couldn't help himself. River was beautiful, even with her tomboyish appeal. Her decline of his advances just made him want her more. After the movie, they went to Lulu's Tacos for dinner. Instead of going inside, they ordered at the drive-thru and ate in the parked car.

Didn't take long for River to scarf down her chicken quesadillas. Andrew finished his bean burrito and grabbed their garbage to throw in a nearby trash bin. When he got back in the car, River was busy scrolling through her phone. Andrew stared at her like a lion eyeing its prey up close. He placed his hand on her thigh, moving his hand back & forth.

"So, where do we go from here?" He asked, making it obvious that he wasn't ready to end their date just yet.

River looked up at him. "Where do we go? Well, I go home. Then you go home."

"Home? But our night is just getting started, you still owe me that kiss remember?"

River placed her hand on top of his. Andrew was hot, there was no denying that. But other than being attracted to him, she had no interest in pursuing any type of relationship with him outside of a casual date. But this didn't mean she couldn't have a little fun. She leaned in and kissed him on the lips. This excited him, and he grabbed her neck and pushed up closer, kissing her back aggressively. He slid his right hand inside of her tank top, caressing her breast from the outside of her bra. He guided his hand over her bra strap and tried to pull it down. Their moment of sexual build-up ended abruptly as River stopped kissing him and pushed away.

"What? What's wrong." Andrew sighed heavily, rubbing his left temple.

"It's not you, I'm just... not feeling this. That's all."

Andrew started to get angry. "Not feeling it? Why not? You were all over me!"

"Drew, I'm just not feeling it. Look, I enjoyed our date, but I'm ready to go home."

Andrew scoffed at her and shook his head. "Tease." He mumbled under his breath.

River shot a look at him. "Excuse me?" She wanted to make sure she had heard him correctly before punching him in the face.

"I asked you out because I think you're sexy as hell. Plus, all the guys at school say you're down."

She raised her left eyebrow. "Down? What is that supposed to mean?"

"Oh, come on. Don't pretend like you don't know what I mean."

"Screw you asshole!" River pushed him in the chest and got out of the car. She slammed the door so hard it could've broken the window. She walked off, furious. He got out of the car to go after her.

"River! River come back!" He yelled. "I didn't mean it!"

She stopped and turned around. "Whatever! Leave me alone! I can get home on my own."

"Really? It's late. You don't have to ever speak to me again, but at least let me take you home. I'm sorry." He looked at her with the face of a pitiful puppy. River was still mad at him, but she wasn't really in the mood to wait around for a ride in a sketchy parking lot. She began to walk toward him, going back to the car. He smiled at her like he always did. That adorable grin on an aggravating boy.

Then it came out of nowhere. A beast, moving so fast she couldn't even blink before Andrew was on the ground, screaming in agony. River became frozen with fear. It was like her feet were glued to the pavement and her legs were made of jelly. The beast ripped at Andrew's torso and bloodshot out like an exploding can of red paint. It was unreal. River's shock ignited her instincts for survival and she ran as fast as she could to the car. Her heart felt like it was about to collapse into her stomach as she yanked at the latch and crawled inside the driver's seat. The keys were still in the ignition. River felt a split moment of relief, that she would be okay. She would live.

The beast smashed through the driver's side window, grabbing River and snatching her through. She screamed as she flew to the ground, her face hitting the pavement, with bits of glass impaled into her skin. She cried out to God to spare her life, but she knew this was the end. The beast pounced on top of her, clawing at her back. Its sharp claws ripping, tearing into her flesh. The horror of being torn to pieces was like nothing she had ever experienced. Her life flashed before her eyes. She saw them, her parents. Their smiling faces welcoming her into the light. She was nine, and happy again. Their faces were the last thing she saw. Followed by the sound of gunshots, before everything went black.

Now available on Amazon!

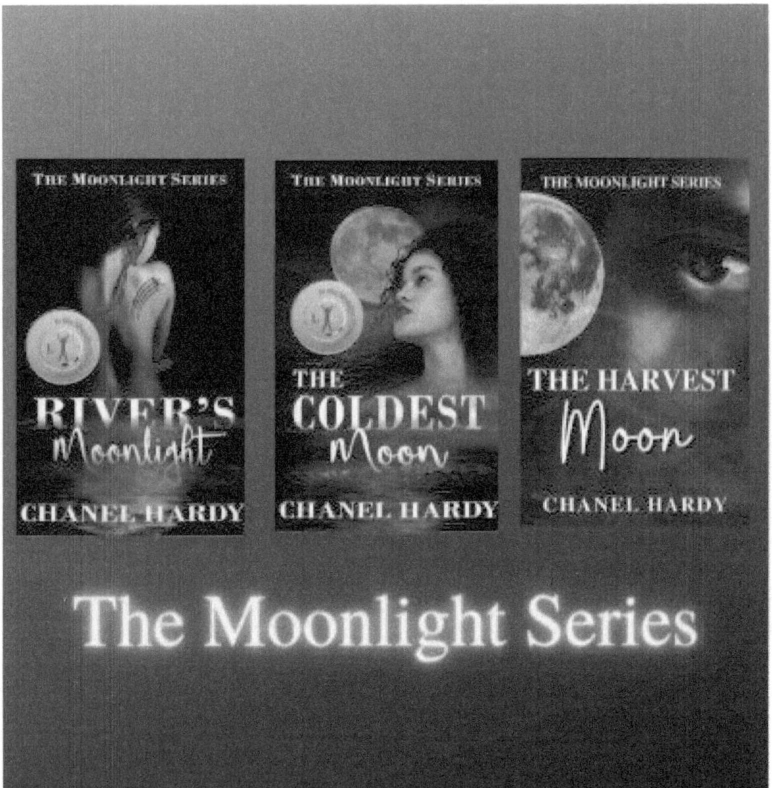

![The Moonlight Series books: River's Moonlight, The Coldest Moon, The Harvest Moon by Chanel Hardy]

The Moonlight Series

Also Check out Hardy Publications Apparel

IG: @hardypubs_apparel
Facebook: Hardypubs Bookish Apparel

Also by Chanel Hardy

About the Author

YA/NA author and poet born and raised in the Washington D.C. area. In 2017 Chanel decided to take a leap of faith and follow her dreams of publishing her first book, 'My Colorblind Rainbow' which made the 'In The Margins Award Long List' for YA fiction in 2018. She launched Hardy Publications in September of 2017, working as a freelance writer and literary blogger. She's written for publications such as Women and Words, 25 Hottest Indie Authors Artists Advocates 2020, and CulEpi. With certifications in persuasive writing and public speaking, TEFL(Teaching English as a Foreign Language) while overseas, Chanel uses her platform to raise awareness for different charities and non-profit organizations, volunteering both locally and internationally, and giving back to the community.

Read more at https://www.chardypublications.com/.

About the Publisher